Cows *and* Horses

BOOKS BY BARBARA WILSON

Novels

Ambitious Women

Murder in the Collective

Sisters of the Road

Stories

Miss Venezuela

Walking on the Moon

Thin Ice

Talk & Contact

Translations

Cora Sandel: Selected Short Stories

Nothing Happened

Cows and Horses

A NOVEL BY
Barbara Wilson

THE EIGHTH MOUNTAIN PRESS

This is a work of fiction; any resemblance of the characters to persons living or dead is purely coincidental. The places in the novel are used fictitiously and the ferry schedule does not correspond to that of the Washington State Ferry System.

Grateful acknowledgment is made for permission to reprint excerpts from the following books:
The People's War: Britain, 1939-1945 by Angus Calder, Pantheon Books; © 1969 by Angus Calder
"On May 30th ... territory." and "Most people ... platforms." reprinted by permission.
Darkness Over Europe by Anthony March, Rand McNally & Co.; © 1969 by Army Times, Inc.
"The people console ... humor." reprinted by permission.
Leningrad Diary by Vera Inber, St. Martin's Press, Inc.; © 1971 by St. Martin's Press, Inc., New York
"16th September ... war." reprinted by permission.
The 900 Days: The Siege of Leningrad by Harrison E. Salisbury, Harper & Row Publishers, Inc.; © 1969 by Harrison E. Salisbury
"The snow ... ice." and "But gradually ... bags." reprinted by permission.

Published by:
The Eighth Mountain Press
624 Southeast 29th Avenue
Portland, Oregon 97214

First Edition
10 9 8 7 6 5 4 3 2 1
Printed in the United States of America

ISBN 0-933377-01-0

Library of Congress Catalog Number: 87-83510

Cover art by Laura Ross-Paul
Cover design by Marcia Barrentine
Book design by Marcia Barrentine and Ruth Gundle

◆ 1 ◆

THERE WAS A TIME LAST FALL WHEN BET WANTED TO GET AWAY for a few days. Norah suggested renting a room from a woman she knew on one of the islands north of Seattle, a woman who ran a small dairy farm and kept a couple of bedrooms in her house for visitors or paying guests. Her name was Mary Anne; Norah had met her at the Vancouver Folk Music Festival two years before. Bet wrote and heard immediately: Yes, one room was free, come anytime.

It was the first week in November, in a season not so much rainy as thoroughly soaked. The sky was a sopping washrag pressed over the broken face of the city. It sounded like nighttime even during the day: the thin, steady weep of rain through dank evergreens, the flattened mush of tires on leaf-thickened asphalt, and everywhere the muted orchestra of illness—sneezing, coughing and complaining.

It was better to leave right away. Bet packed a suitcase, threw extra sweaters and shoes and books into the back of her car and headed north. Soon the claustrophobic terrarium around Puget Sound gave way to the lowering Dutch skies of the Skagit Valley, with its lonely farms and pastures, its single lines of windblown, leafless trees. Bet drove onto the ferry at Anacortes and went upstairs to the cafeteria as they slipped into the damp, mournful mists of Rosario Strait. She didn't go out on the deck once, but stayed curled inside on a leatherette seat, drinking Earl Grey tea with milk from her thermos.

There weren't many passengers. It was mid-week in the off-season. They would, as Norah said, still remain friends.

Mary Anne was a solid woman, with great firm arms and broad shoulders under a blue turtleneck and navy wool shirt. She was a little older than Bet, in her late thirties, early forties perhaps. Her hair was roan red with fine threads of silver; it grew past her shoulders, full of hundreds of tiny waves, as if it had just been released from tight braids. Her face was so heavily freckled that the features were hard to see at first; the backs of her work-toughened hands were like the skins of spotted animals.

She shook Bet's hand at the door, then, seeing her hungry face, drew her in from the early dark with its mulched fragrance of earth and trees and gave her a hug, hard and floury.

"Come into the kitchen while I finish making dinner. No difficulty finding the place, I hope? You look exhausted, bless your heart."

Bet knew she was going to like it here. The kitchen was lit by oil lamps that swung from the low ceiling and hung along the sides of the darkened cedar walls. There was a red tile floor with a rag rug, and a wood fire in the stove. It smelled of bread and soup and everything that Bet was longing for: security, goodness, peace.

Mary Anne gave her tea, moving around the kitchen with a light step. She had a body like a ship's figurehead, robust torso, long slender legs. "Make yourself at home," she kept saying. "We'll be eating in, say, half an hour, if that's all right with you . . . my daughter Tam is just out finishing up the milking now."

"So Norah wasn't joking then—about your herd of cows?"

"Hardly a herd, not with six Guernseys. But it's a start, and with the goat and the chickens, it's plenty for now, enough." Mary Anne was chopping carrots, throwing the stumpy orange chunks into a red enamel pot. "Enough to live," she added. "We do odd jobs, canning, have a truck farm—and we rent out part of the pasture. There's a woman in Anacortes who keeps two horses there, comes over on weekends . . . .You'll meet her if you stay awhile."

Mary Anne paused and looked over at Bet. Her eyes were frank and warm, like two bits of chocolate just starting to melt; between her fingers were leeks, transparent as chips of milky green glass. They hadn't yet discussed terms or the length of Bet's stay. "Are you on vacation or . . . ?"

"Just a short break. Norah and I are still running the futon business. Flexible Futons." She made a weak joke, "We try to be flexible, too."

Mary Anne smiled. She sat down at the heavy oak table across from Bet. "I haven't seen Norah now for a couple of years, ever since the music festival. How is she?"

"Just fine," said Bet, tight-lipped in a way Mary Anne couldn't fail to notice. But Mary Anne didn't ask anything more, only picked up a wrinkled yellow and red apple from an earthenware bowl; holding it in her fingers she unwrapped its peel with a single movement of her knife, a smooth arc. She said cheerfully,

"I don't get to Seattle more than once a year now. In fact, I don't get off the island much since I started keeping all the animals."

Bet reached for a curl of peel and chewed on its grainy sweetness. "You've always lived in the country?" she asked, to say something.

Mary Anne smiled at her. The skin around her eyes crinkled like late fall apples; she sliced the naked white fruit rhythmically. "No, I grew up in San Jose, lived in Berkeley in the late sixties, kept moving north." She turned her strong torso and pointed the knife in the direction of the window, a rectangle of blue-black in the wooden wall. "We bought land up here when it was cheap. Jack fished."

She was matter-of-fact. Norah had said that Jack drowned, fishing, and that Mary Anne had been left without much of anything. There had only been enough in the small life insurance policy to pay off the land.

A girl of eleven or twelve came into the kitchen, bringing with her the smell of wet manure and animals. She'd taken off her boots in the entryway; her stockinged feet slid over the floor to her mother's side. She hardly looked at Bet, but grabbed an apple slice from the plate on the table and leaned into the arm that went around her.

"I took Kelly's horses some carrots, Mom. They're starting to really recognize me—well, Nutmeg is. I can hardly wait till Kelly comes again. I don't see why I can't ride Nutmeg when Kelly's not here. Kelly said I had a good seat, she said I was a natural, remember? A natural-born rider. Don't you think we can ask her when she comes if I can ride during the week, Mom?"

Tam had short chestnut curls and pale strawberry freckles. She was thin and shooting up quickly; flat-chested, broad-shouldered, she was almost as tall as Mary Anne. The sleeves of her sweater no longer reached her wrists.

"Kelly's been teaching Tam to ride." Mary Anne tried to pull down one of the sweater sleeves, then moved to put the apple crisp in the oven. "It's been Tammy's dream for years."

"*Can't* we ask Kelly when she comes? *Please*? Is she coming this weekend?" Tam followed her mother and hung on one of her arms.

"You know better than to ask when she's coming," Mary Anne smiled, then sighed. "Everybody knows that Kelly turns up when Kelly decides to turn up."

After dinner mother and daughter cleared up together, insisting that Bet stay right where she was, then Tam settled down to homework at the big oak table and Mary Anne showed Bet her room. It was simple and comfortable, like the rest of the house, with a white iron bedstead and a quilt. On the wall was a painting of horses in a pasture. There was a row of pegs for Bet's clothes on the door and a wooden night table with a little lamp.

Bet sat down on the bed. "This is fine. This is just exactly what I needed."

Mary Anne sat down beside her and gave her an impulsive hug. She smelled of yeast and apples and she had large breasts, not full and round like Norah's but low and massive, firmly held in.

"I hope you'll get a good rest here," Mary Anne said, and her voice was warm with sympathy. "You look like you need one."

It was an opening for Bet to spill her troubles if she wanted to. She didn't. She looked over at the painting of horses on the wall.

"Somehow I don't remember going through a horse phase when I was a kid."

"I didn't either," Mary Anne said. "Actually, I thought the girls who did were pretty strange. And now here's Tam. She was more than fanatic enough about it before Kelly came on the scene." Mary Anne propped herself up on the pillows and began to braid a length of crinkled hair. "First it was reading girl-and-her-horse books from the library, then collecting pictures from calendars and magazines. Last summer she started talking about riding lessons. And now that we've actually got some horses around, she can't keep away from them. Rushes home from school just to stare at them. One night in the middle of a thunderstorm I woke up and she wasn't in her bed. She was out in the barn, talking to the horses so they wouldn't be scared, she said." Mary Anne unwove the strand of hair and flung it back on her shoulder with a laugh. "She lives for Kelly's visits."

"Tell me about Kelly. What's she like?"

Mary Anne considered. "Interesting. Complicated. She doesn't say a lot about herself, and then it comes out she's done something amazing, like sailing alone to Puerto Rico, or that she knows all about sheep shearing in Tuscany or sugaring-off in Vermont. I don't know her all that well really . . . it's only been a couple of months, since September, that she's been keeping her horses here."

Bet shifted away slightly; there was something about Mary Anne that was too familiar. "What's she do? I mean, for a living?"

"She's a welder at the Texaco refinery outside Anacortes. You couldn't have missed it on the way to the ferry. Kelly lives in Anacortes somewhere. I can't imagine why, it's so ugly. Maybe she likes it. She's a little wild . . . but you'll see." Mary Anne pulled a loose thread on the quilt and snapped it off. "Pretty intense sometimes. I suspect a lot of burned bridges behind her."

"She sounds like a dangerous woman."

Mary Anne laughed. "Mostly dangerous to herself, I think . . . .Well," Mary Anne pushed off slowly from the bed. "If you need anything, just ask."

Bet wished she could.

Two days went by, warm inside, brisk out, with flurries of rain and wind. Mary Anne was up at five every morning to feed and milk the cows. Afterwards she cooked breakfast for Tam and made sure she got off to school. Later in the morning Mary Anne cleaned the shed and milking stalls, fed the bantams and the geese, gathered the eggs, fed the goat and the horses. In the afternoon she bottled

the raw milk for her neighbors and customers, delivered
the milk and the eggs, cleaned the house, made bread,
shopped if necessary, cooked dinner and did the evening
milking with Tam. In the evening she knit sweaters of angora that were sold for high prices in the island boutique.

Bet did nothing. Nothing useful anyway.

The air around the farm was manure-heavy, not
unpleasant. The cows were usually in a small pasture near
the house, as if they liked the company. They kept near
each other, grazing on what grass they could find and
steaming heavily when it rained. They were odd, patient
animals, angular bones competing with ballooning stom-
achs, and their amazingly large ugly slow faces with their
beautiful long-lashed eyes turned in wonder on Bet as she
passed. The horses were in another pasture. They bent
their heads to the grass and their curved necks were
lovely and fluid, like brown and copper fountains running
into the ground.

Twice a day Bet went out for a walk, down the country
lanes and less traveled roads. This island was inward-
looking, with few roads by the water. It was farmland,
quiet and prosaic. The fields were fallow now, dark loamy
brown, sometimes with the broken stalks of the harvest
strewn over them like cake decorations. The pastures
were yellow-green and spotty, surrounded by a brush of
russet and ochre and forests of bluish firs. There were
horses and cows everywhere and Bet liked the way they
looked at her—thoughtfully, as if trying to remember
where they'd met.

Most of the day, however, she read by the wood stove
or under her quilt in the bedroom. She was reading

history, trying to catch up. She'd never understood the twentieth century the way she felt she should.

Lately she had been reading about the Second World War in Europe. Not the battles, but how it was to live in Paris during the occupation, or London during the Blitz. What it was like to be an evacuee, a refugee, a bare survivor. She was interested in the everyday life of people who suffered momentous change: what they ate, what they wore, how they entertained themselves.

At the moment she was deep in a blow by blow account of the home front in England, living in a secret imaginary world of ration books and utility cloth, a world where people slept in the subways and banged into each other in the streets during the blackout, a world where London was bombed for seventy-six nights in a row during the fall of 1941, except for November 2, when there was bad weather.

Sometimes in the evenings, she and Mary Anne talked. They talked about the farm, about animals, about running a business. Mary Anne talked about her life with Jack, about the woman who had left her to go work in Alaska and who hadn't come back, about Judy, her current lover, about raising a daughter.

Bet listened mostly, and watched the silver needles weave through the soft autumn shades of angora. She felt peaceful here, useless but safe.

They never talked about Norah.

◆ ◆ ◆

On Friday afternoon Mary Anne asked if Bet would like to go to the village delicatessen with her. That was where Judy worked, and Mary Anne wanted to ask her to dinner Saturday night. They drove in Bet's car.

A cloudy day was different here from the city, where gray turned the skyscrapers and the streets monolithic and oppressive. On the island the gray sky was large, translucent, shifting ceaselessly like water in the middle of the ocean, with nothing to break against. And yet this gray couldn't rob the trees and land of their colors; nothing leached or bled here. Instead, contrasts grew and sharpened.

"When Jack and I moved here . . . ," Mary Anne stopped. "You must be tired of hearing about him. I'm sorry."

"Don't be," said Bet. "It's not hard to understand . . . a person gets under your skin. I mean, if you're together a long time . . . ."

Bet felt Mary Anne looking at her, considering whether or not to probe. "I like how everyone waves here, when they go by in their cars," Bet said hastily. "It's very homey, isn't it?"

Judy was standing behind the counter of the deli when they came in. She was slender, taller than both of them, wearing a white apron over her sweatshirt and jeans. Her black hair was very short; her dark blue eyes alive and quizzical behind thick glasses.

"Judy Journeywoman," Mary Anne introduced them. "This is Bet Gallagher from Seattle. Bet's staying with us for a few days."

"Hi," said Judy. She had a beautifully cut mouth and an open, quite earnest expression. She came around the counter and faced Mary Anne. "I've run into a snag with my book—can we talk about it sometime soon?"

"That's why we're here," said Mary Anne. "I wanted you to come to dinner tomorrow night."

"But will we be able to talk?" Judy played with a stray lock of Mary Anne's hair, as if drawn to its fiery color.

Mary Anne shrugged her off. "Of course we can talk. Maybe Kelly will be there too. You can try out some of your theories on her."

"But she doesn't know anything about feminist theory; she's practically illiterate, as far as I can tell." Judy turned enthusiastically to Bet, "I'm spooking a chapter for a book I'm writing. Are you connected to the university?"

"I'm not that connected to anything right now."

"Don't be silly," said Mary Anne. "Bet is part owner of a futon shop in Seattle. She's a capitalist, like me."

"Mary Anne, I've told you—that doesn't concern me. I'm not into socialist-feminism. I'm not interested in *economics.*" Bet and Mary Anne couldn't help grinning at each other, and Judy, hearing herself, gave a dry little laugh, "Well you know what I mean."

"I wish I weren't," said Mary Anne, giving Judy a pat. "Must be nice."

Back in the car Mary Anne said, "You can't take her too seriously, you know. She's really sweet."

"What did she mean, spooking a chapter?"

"I think that's Dalyese for writing an expose. You know—spooking, sparking and spinning? She's really into

Mary Daly, she even got me to read *Pure Lust*." Mary Anne frowned doubtfully. "She's highly intelligent—but sometimes I wish she wouldn't talk so much. It puts me in a motherly mood—in the beginning I used to feel more passion."

"How old is she?"

Mary Anne looked uncomfortable.

"Twenty-two." When Bet didn't say anything, she went on, "It's not easy to find lovers on the island."

"I can't imagine that it would be." Bet was watching the sky surge above the horizon, watching how the field changed color, like a reversible coat when the wind blew, from pale white gold to sable.

"I knew you were mad," said Mary Anne suddenly. "But if you were mad, why did you come to stay?"

"What?"

"About Norah. About Norah and me that time. But it was two years ago, it was just a night or two. It was nothing."

"It was nothing," Bet repeated mechanically.

"Well, you knew, didn't you? Didn't Norah tell you?"

Bet kept driving. "No," she said. "But it doesn't matter. Really, Mary Anne, it doesn't matter now."

That evening, just after dinner, Bet called Norah from a pay phone in the village. She was, somewhat unexpectedly, at home. At her home. She'd moved out of theirs two weeks ago.

"Hi," said Norah, her voice encouraging and warm. "How is it up there? How's Mary Anne? Are you enjoying yourself?"

Yesterday Bet would have been prepared to tell her how much she was enjoying herself, how she thought she was recovering, how everything might be okay. Now she heard her voice cold and subdued. "It's fine, just fine. How are you?"

"Oh, great." Norah chattered for a moment about the sales and orders and outlined the details of a custom job. All Bet could think of was her mouth on Mary Anne's, her mouth on Eleanor's now.

"I'm surprised you're home," she found herself saying. "After all, it's Friday night."

"Checking up on me again?" Norah shot back. But she didn't sound upset. "We're going out later . . . Bet, don't do this . . . ."

"I'm sorry. I don't know why I do it."

"I don't know why either," and her voice was low. "You know I love you. I'll always love you."

Bet didn't believe her. "I love you too."

Norah hmm'd gently and then the briskness came, the horrible, inevitable briskness. "I was thinking that while you were gone it would be a good time to maybe clear out some more of my stuff. You know, the kitchen things I didn't get, those two plants and—"

"Oh sure, go ahead. You've still got the key. Take whatever you want."

"Bet, you know I forgot some things . . . I was just thinking, it might be easier while you—"

"Look, I said, take whatever you want."

"How's Mary Anne?" Norah asked again. And then, when Bet didn't answer, "I wish I knew why you called me."

"Because I wanted to talk to you," Bet said, and laughed grimly.

Norah laughed too. "So now we've talked. So I'll see you next week. Monday or Tuesday or whatever. All right? We'll talk some more then."

"Sure. Okay, fine. Well, see you."

Norah's sigh wavered between compassion and frustration, but a soft "Bye," was all she said.

◆2◆

THE NEXT DAY BET STAYED AWAY FROM THE FARM, STARTING
out early on a long walk that took her around the circumference of the island, as near to the shore as possible. The
temperature was in the mild fifties; it often appeared that
the sun was going to break through, but it never did. The
sky looked like a badly made bed, piled with dark pillows
and ragged lengths of sheeting, and finally it rained. Bet
picnicked under her poncho on one beach, had tea from
her thermos on another.

The water ebbed back through the stones like the sea
brushing her hair; wherever Bet stood, whichever side of
the island, she could see the other islands in the chain
huddled nearby, like sleeping animals of the same family,
a dark green breed thickly furred with evergreens.

She returned around four to find a black Triumph
parked in Mary Anne's driveway. There were two figures

in the pasture with the horses. Bet went up to the fence and waved.

Tam shouted, "Bet, Bet. We've been riding the *horses*. I learned to *canter,* want to see?"

The woman with her came over to Bet, walking carefully, with a swagger so deliberate as to be almost a mince. "Kelly Astor," she said, and shook Bet's hand over the fence. Bet registered a stronger than usual grasp and didn't know whether she liked it or not. Kelly was smaller than she was, but with the rigid bearing of a cadet. Her hair, short, coarse, black-brown with a few strands of white, was cut back sharply over her ears but sprang from her crown like a nest of frayed electrical cords. At the moment her features made little impression on Bet; it was only when she let go of Kelly's hand that she had the unexpected sensation of wanting it back.

"Nice horses," Bet said.

Kelly nodded seriously in their direction, where a delighted Tam was feeding Nutmeg a carrot. "Do you ride?"

"No."

"I'd be glad to teach you." Kelly's eyes were dark hazel, her skin chapped and thin. One of her front teeth bumped crookedly into the other and left a gap next to it; it gave her smile a faintly pugilistic air.

"I guess I'll just watch for now," Bet said.

Kelly nodded and turned, painstakingly making her way back across the soggy, pitted pasture. She had a Levi jacket on over a heavy cable sweater, tight jeans, a silky red scarf. Bet absorbed all the details now: a little bow-legged, well-defined thighs and buttocks.

You're not going to act on this, she told herself. She's trouble. Bet liked the way that sounded somehow. She said it again, aloud, but softly, leaning on the rail fence, looking at Kelly. "She's trouble."

Tam, curls squashed under a baseball cap, navy sweater under a windbreaker and knee warmers pulled up high so that her pants ballooned out like old-fashioned jodphurs, couldn't help bouncing up and down on Nutmeg's saddle. "Gee-up," she cried out. "Come on, old Nutmeg you. We can do it. We can win the Grand National."

"Careful now," Kelly called. She had mounted the other horse, a glossy young animal with a black mane and a high, nervous step. "Don't yank the reins, Tam, you'll hurt her mouth. Guide her gently, she'll follow you."

The rain had stopped some time ago and now the canopy of the sky was lightening, as if the clouds were sinking like heavy sediment to the bottom of the horizon. All around the pasture the clouds formed a dark-blue band above and behind the thrusting greenery of the firs and mountain ash. The earth gave off a smell of mulched-down leaves, and there was a smokiness in the air—wood burning in fireplaces and stoves around the island. Sounds carried: Kelly's encouraging instructions, Tam's punctuating cries of excitement, birds, the ferry's horn, the speaking silence of the ground and trees.

Bet was suddenly conscious of how still she was standing, as if she were holding her breath, as if she were photographing a moment that required total concentration and total stillness.

Mary Anne came out from the house, wearing a rubber apron and heavy boots. Her red rippled hair fell to her shoulders under a headband. "Thought I'd do the milking myself this afternoon," she said a little awkwardly when she saw Bet standing at the fence. "It's a shame to interrupt Tam when she's having such a good time."

"Can I help?"

"Sure."

They brought the six cows into the shed. They were bigger than ever close up and they had horns that Bet hadn't noticed before. She watched out for their hooves and their tails and touched them gingerly, while Mary Anne pushed and whacked them into place and called them by their names: Fiona, Poppie, Lydia, Loretta, Jewel and Dolly.

"Come on, girls, into the boudoir. You know," Mary Anne told Bet, "on the larger farms they call these sheds milking parlors—no, I'm serious. Not that they have doilies on the troughs or anything; they usually put the cows on a kind of conveyer belt and keep them moving." She led Lydia and Fiona over to the stanchions and put their heads through, locking them into position. She took a canful of grain from a wooden barrel and tossed it into the trough in front of them. They bent their heads and ate.

"Parlor," laughed Mary Anne. "I bet Judy and Mary Daly would have something to say about that." She was nervous and kept talking. "I still milk by hand, since I've only got six. You can milk a cow in ten or fifteen minutes if you're fairly strong. Most places these days use vacuum pumps though."

She fetched warm water from the other room and came back to wash the cows' teats, then brought out a stainless steel bucket and began on Fiona. "See," she explained to Bet, "first you pull, you've got to get it going, pull and squeeze, pull and squeeze, umm, isn't that nice, Fiona?"

Fiona didn't pause in her chewing, but Lydia looked around with big, apprehensive eyes when Bet took an exploratory pull at her. "Uh, it's okay, Lydia," she said, feeling foolish. "Just give me a minute to get started." Lydia shifted and stared and finally mooed at Bet, who was finding it harder than it looked. The teat was stiff and thick; it was oddly like pulling on someone's finger. Finally she got some milk and invented a small rhythm that brought more. The yellowish fluid splashed into the bucket, looking very different than it did coming out of the carton at home.

"I felt bad, well, not bad, but awkward, about what happened yesterday," said Mary Anne, over the steady plunk and squirt of milk.

Bet, prepared for this, said, "Don't."

The barn was as dim as an old church and late afternoon light shimmered in through the small-paned windows as if Teniers had captured it in oils of pale jonquil and burnt umber. The cows shifted quietly and chewed.

"You know," said Bet, willing herself, if not to be open, then to be honest. "Norah and I broke up two weeks ago. For good, I mean."

"You'd been together a long time."

"Ten years. But—she has someone else now. No, it's all right. It had been coming for a while."

"I'm sorry," said Mary Anne. "She spoke very highly of you; she said she was happy. I don't know how it happened, it was just—"

"Some years ago," said Bet firmly, "I asked Norah not to tell me any more what she did . . . she usually did anyway. So I suppose I have the feeling that I knew all about, about all the times . . . Anyway, it doesn't matter now. Really, it doesn't."

"But—"

"I'd like to change the subject. There's nothing more to say."

Mary Anne had more to say, Bet knew that. She would have liked to confide, to commiserate, to hear the sordid details, to finally suggest, like all their friends, with just a hint of malice, that she'd known two years ago. Or five years ago. Or ten. That Bet and Norah would split up someday, were bound to. Because Norah, after all, was a restless person, and would never be satisfied to spend the rest of her life with one lover. That she had managed ten years with Bet was a miracle really; it had only happened because Bet was blind and blindly forgiving.

But Mary Anne did change the subject, peaceably, whether or not she was satisfied that they'd come to any conclusion. "I don't know why, but I really like cows. I like how they're such creatures of habit. They don't enjoy change, they want everything exactly the same, day after day, week after week . . . ."

"Month after month, year after year," Bet finished and they laughed. "Yes, I can understand that."

Judy Journeywomon was in the kitchen, scribbling at the big oak table when they came in.

"It's so dark in here," Mary Anne said. "How can you write in the dark?" She sailed around lighting the oil lamps, checking the stove and adding wood. "You should have put another log on, it's freezing in here . . . Well, never mind, we'll soon get it warmed up and I'll put the lasagne in the oven and make dessert."

Judy yawned and blinked as she raised her eyes from her notebook to smile at Mary Anne and receive her kiss. She looked fifteen, a teenager in a baggy sweatshirt and jeans.

"I've started the new chapter," she announced cheerfully. "I'm going to question the whole concept of tenure."

"Tenure?" said Mary Anne. "Where? In women's studies, or just in general?"

"In general, at those nexuses of necrophilia, but especially in women's studies. Crones with their own croneology competing for cowardly crumbs." Judy coughed her dry little laugh.

"Judy was having an affair with one of her women's studies professors," Mary Anne told Bet. "I think she's still working it out."

"Mary Anne, that's not true," Judy protested. "I'm spinning the whole subject. There are much larger issues involved." She turned to Bet. "Do you know Jocelyn Edwards?"

Bet shook her head.

Judy looked disappointed. "Well, she was my professor. Actually, she's not that well known. She probably will be, though, the way she's climbing all over herself."

"I'm not that up on who's who in—" Bet started to explain, but Judy interrupted,

"We started being lovers at the beginning of my senior year, about a year ago. I never thought of myself as particularly younger or less experienced. I'd been a lesbian all my life; *she'd* been married once, a member of NOW, things like that . . . and her interest was in Victorian women's literature . . . I was the one who made her read Mary Daly, I mean, really read her—a lot of people just pretend they've read her, you know." Judy darted a quick glance at Bet.

"And we read some brilliant French women too. Cixous, Irigaray, Wittig—women doing things with language, reinventing language from the perspective of women. But then," and Judy's lovely mouth twisted at the corners, "we went to the National Women's Studies Conference. I'd graduated by then, there was no reason to keep it quiet anymore. But Jocelyn was still nervous about it, she didn't want to share a room or anything. And then I found out why."

Judy's voice grew low and driving. She drummed rhythmically on the table with her pencil, banging out the words as if she were typing. "She'd started having an affair, that's why, with one of the really big names, one of those really *big* women's studies names who's published all the time in *Signs* and by university presses, boring sociological stuff, with male-referenced, foot-bound footnotes everywhere, a socialist-feminist. All Jocelyn was really interested in was advancing herself in women's studies. I couldn't help her do that, oh no, at the conference I was just another young, radical lesbian feminist in jeans, and Jocelyn was a professor with professional contacts, talking about curriculum and mainstreaming and *tenure*. Tenure, as if that should spell anything but defeat, getting accepted by them— when she'd even been talking herself about the university being nothing but a temple of necrophilia. And then she gets involved with this *fembot*, this woman wearing tweed jackets and narrow ties!"

Mary Anne came over to her and put her arms around Judy's shoulders. "Oh Judy, let's not think about it right now, okay? Your book's going to be wonderful, I know it is, it's such an exciting topic—education."

Tears dripped from Judy's dark blue eyes as she sought to lay a cause to her unhappiness. "But it's so hard!" She finally managed. "There are no good *libraries* on the island."

Mary Anne looked over at Bet. "Do you think you could go and see what Kelly and Tam are up to? Tell them dinner will be in half an hour or so."

Bet put her boots back on in the entryway and took her down jacket. It was dark outside now, dark the way it gets in the country, with no lights lifting up the horizon. She thought of Judy's last words. Libraries, where she often liked to go at night, seemed far away now, in cities where people were walking around, going out to dinner, coming home from work, stopping at the grocery store. She felt for the first time what it meant to be on an island, a configuration of land surrounded by water, dark water and a black sky with stars up above.

Two circles of light came towards her from the barn.

"Bet, Bet," said Tam, sprinting forward with her flashlight. "Kelly says Glory could be a racehorse with some training. She says maybe I could ride her in a race."

Kelly came up to the porch more slowly. "Glory feels like a jumper to me. I just hope she doesn't start trying to jump over the fence."

"Why do you keep them here?" Bet asked. "Instead of nearer to where you live. Anacortes, isn't it?"

"Whim," and Bet sensed her smiling in the darkness. "Or maybe I like to keep separate parts of myself separate. When the horses were near me in the Skagit Valley I used to spend too much of my life with them. This way, I only see them a few times a month."

"Don't take them away," Tam begged. "Or, or—I'll buy them, if you don't want them."

"I didn't say I didn't want them," said Kelly, and now Bet could see her smile with its crooked tooth behind the flashlight's flicker. "But even things you love you need distance from sometimes. You'll understand that someday."

Tam ran to the door. "I'll never feel that way, never in a million years!" she threw back before she went inside.

Bet and Kelly laughed.

"Are you involved with anyone?" Kelly asked, with no change of tone.

Bet said nothing. She looked at the stars.

"Yes, then," Kelly murmured. "Oh well."

"No, then."

"Good." Kelly moved as if to go inside, but Bet couldn't leave it like that.

"Some parts of it are still going on, most of it is over." She felt Kelly waiting. "We're in business together. We're trying to be friends . . . ."

She was silent suddenly and Kelly laughed. "The curse of the serial monogamists—friendship afterwards. I make it a point never to be friends."

Bet laughed too, uneasily. "I'll remember that."

They went inside.

"Judy wants us to talk about college during dinner," Mary Anne said, taking the lasagne out of the oven. "She wants our college experiences for her book."

"What *is* your book?" Bet asked.

"It's called *Elemental Education*, or I might call it *Gyn/ucation* with the emphasis on 'new'. It's about un-learning in the Phallic State." Judy said this with an air of resolution. Her eyes were still a little red behind the thick glasses.

"Why not?" asked Kelly. She leaned back in her chair and rocked slightly. She was not a good-looking woman, Bet thought, disappointed. The shape of her face was too round, its color pasty white, with reddened cheeks. The eyes were smallish and the eyelids puffy. Then Kelly turned and her aquiline profile broke Bet's heart.

"Why not?" Kelly repeated, looking at Mary Anne. "Mary Anne can tell us all about the good old days in Berkeley."

"Oh Mom," said Tam. "Don't tell the same stories. All those marches."

Mary Anne put the salad on the table and sat down. She had taken off her headband and her wrinkly hair was gathered up carelessly. Two large gold hoops caught the light from the oil lamps. "Someday you'll be begging me to recreate the late sixties for your high school oral history project."

"Is it possible," said Bet, "that they'll be teaching the sixties, that they're history now?"

"History didn't just happen before you were born," said Kelly, with a wink.

Bet hated winking. "Go on, Mary Anne," she said politely.

Mary Anne told them about studying sociology and political science, about working against the draft, about the Black Panthers and SDS. "Jack was keeping out of Vietnam, so we just went on and on going to college, got our masters, started our doctorates—but by then the days of revolution had come and gone . . . I started taking pottery and Indian cookery classes, and Jack was learning carpentry and stained glass . . . and then we thought about agricultural school or even a zen monastery, but we ended up moving to Oregon and then up here to the island."

"Were you aware of the women's movement?" Judy asked, trying to take Mary Anne's hand.

Mary Anne drew it away. "I'd have to say no, not really. But of course I was, on all sorts of levels. It just didn't sink in. I was married, and had mostly married friends, and we all thought of ourselves as progressive as hell. Though, if anything, we were assbackwards about a lot of things. If anyone had talked to me about my oppression then, about the oppression of women, I would have felt they were wrong, about me anyway. I was strong, loving, beautiful, nurturing, you know, all that!"

"You still are," said Kelly gallantly, and this time Bet saw her winking at Mary Anne. No, she decided, she could never have an affair with a woman who winked.

"Maybe," said Mary Anne, "maybe . . . but at the time there was no stigma attached to it . . . I see myself in my long India print dress, barefoot, with a baby in a backpack . . . ."

Tam looked interested. "That was me, wasn't it?"

"Of course, who else?" Mary Anne gave her a hug from the side. "But we're getting off the subject. You're younger, aren't you, Bet? I guessed you missed some of that involvement, though no, you would have been an undergraduate . . . ."

"I would have," said Bet, fighting the old embarrassment. "I never went to college."

There was a slight, surprised silence, then Mary Anne rushed on, "Well, that was very much the times too. Everyone was dropping out. The university wasn't seen then as a job factory, I mean, it was a way of getting out of the draft for men, and for women—"

"No," said Bet. "It wasn't like that. I—I wasn't all that great in school. My mother wanted me out of the house, she wanted me to get married, but I just moved in with a friend and got a job. I had to."

Only Kelly looked at her as if she had any notion of what that might have been like. Judy appeared quite shocked and Mary Anne said, consolingly, "Well, lots of people did that too, of course."

"Oh, it wasn't so bad. I had kind of an interesting job, worked for a Chinese guy in his import business in Los Angeles. He was pretty nutty, but I liked him. I was always going to learn Chinese, just to surprise him one day, but of course I never did. I had a boyfriend who worked there too, in the warehouse."

Bet stopped, then went on. "Anyway, once I moved up to Seattle I took a few classes here and there, played around with the idea of going to the university and getting a degree, but . . . I don't know. I'd been out of school so long and I'd never really enjoyed it . . . and then I met Norah and we started the business. Well, that's it really."

"I never liked school either," Kelly said matter-of-factly. "But in my family, you just went. They tried to get me into a private college, but at least I resisted that. I went to the University of Connecticut. It wasn't so bad. I used to go down to New York on the weekends, go to the bars."

She rocked back in her chair and again winked at Bet. This time Bet didn't look away.

"I've read about that period," Judy said, anthropologically. "I mean, the bar scene. Beebo Brinker, all that stuff."

"I studied art," said Kelly, ignoring her. "I went to Italy—Florence and Rome—for a year after graduation, then I came back and worked in a gallery."

The image of Kelly in a New York art gallery was so unexpected that Bet couldn't help laughing. "Did you wear dresses and everything?"

"Of course not," Kelly reprimanded her. "I wore tight black Levis and an oxford shirt and sometimes a tie or a turtleneck, and I slicked my hair back. This wasn't uptown, it was the Village, and the gallery owner was my lover."

Tam leaned forward with interest. "Did she give you a horse?" she asked, with the logic of the single-minded child.

Bet wondered how Tam could be so certain it was a she.

"She did indeed," said Kelly, finishing off the rest of her lasagne. "She had a farm in Vermont. We used to go there in the summers."

"What happened to the horse?" Tam wanted to know.

"It died. And that's my college story," Kelly said abruptly, and got up to clear the table.

"Well," said Judy, somewhat puzzled. "Thanks for sharing." She added cheerfully, "You know, I just realized you didn't even *have* women's studies back then."

After dinner they sat in the living room and watched *The Birds* on television. Mary Anne knitted one of her fragile angora sweaters while Judy criticized Hitchcock's view of women's sexuality. "Tippie's punished whenever she has a sexual thought—those ugly black birds just come flying at her, pecking at her with their beaks, look at that."

"Please Judy," said Mary Anne, looking at Tam.

Kelly said nothing much all evening, but went out three or four times to "get a breath of fresh air." Each time she looked at Bet before she left the room, but Bet couldn't think of a reason to follow her.

They all went to bed early.

That night Bet dreamed she was standing alone in a pasture; she had some of the accouterments of riding, not all. One riding boot, not two; a saddle, but no reins. She was looking for her horse when she saw Kelly coming towards her, walking slowly across the field. Bet stood there, then started walking too, towards Kelly. But it was like a slapstick western; just as they got near each other, a horse and rider came barreling down on them. She and Kelly stepped back to let the horse through. Norah was riding it, hair wild, face set in a terrible exhilaration. She raced by without looking at Bet or Kelly and was gone, leaping over fences as if they were matchsticks.

"She's a jumper all right," Bet heard Kelly say.

Bet woke up late the next morning and found that Kelly had gone back to Anacortes on the early ferry.

"She gets restless," said Mary Anne. "I saw her when I was coming back from milking the cows. Six a.m. and there she was, putting on her helmet. Tam's disappointed, of course. She lives for those horses."

It was raining, slowly and heavily, like clear snow. The morning dragged by. Judy pored through books and dictionaries, occasionally calling out a particularly interesting etymology, scribbling in her notebook at the kitchen table, making herself endless cups of tea. She'd gotten a cold and kept sneezing. Mary Anne fed the fire in the living room and went on knitting, occasionally pushing her hair back from her face.

Tam was reading an engrossing story about a girl who used her horse to give rides to blind children, and Bet was reading about the phony war in Britain.

On May 30th, it was ordered that "no person shall display or cause or permit to be displayed any sign which furnishes any indication of the name of, or the situation or the direction of, or the distance to any place." Signposts and street names were removed . . . The armed forces themselves soon requested a partial restoration of signs, and boards were erected with vague slogans like "To the South-West," but drivers were still subjected to bafflement and nervous exhaustion if they ventured into unfamiliar territory.

At one o'clock Bet suddenly got up and said, "Well, I think it's time for me to get back to Seattle. I keep forgetting tomorrow's Monday and work. Vacation's over."

Mary Anne gave her a loaf of bread and some homemade preserves. As Bet left she said, "I hope everything goes all right, with you and Norah . . . ."

And she invited Bet to come back and stay any time.

·*3*·

LIKE A DUTCH PAINTING FROM THE EARLY SEVENTEENTH century the colors of a November morning in Seattle were drab and unified, matte with no sudden shafts of light. Bet parked by the Ship Canal in Fremont on her way to work Monday and stood for a while wondering how to meet Norah, what to say. Poplars lined the canal banks and hid the industrial buildings and warehouses; in late fall the trees were stripped and thin, brushing with tight, unspreading limbs the barely blue morning sky. A fine white mist hovered, and through it, squat tugs pulled barges loaded with logs and pyramids of sand and gravel. There were times when Bet had seen an entire house, windows empty and expectant, slip by, on its way to a lot on the other side of Lake Washington.

In spite of her delay Bet arrived before Norah; she walked through the store to the office in back as through a place she'd never been. She marveled uneasily at the luxury of the holiday stock, newly arrived: tatami mats, rice paper and matchstick bamboo shades, pillows of polished cotton, light pine sofa and bed frames, paper lampshades, lacquered black boxes and fabrics printed with peonies and chrysanthemums. Lanterns hung above, glowing with soft light; the matting on the floor was noiseless and thick. As if for the first time Bet understood just how much the look of the store reflected Norah: discreet, practical, delicately beautiful.

The bulky padded futons, the beginning and mainstay of their business, were suspended in rows from wooden dowels, safely out of the way.

Norah came in just as Bet reached the coffeemaker in back.

"You're home," she called. "Welcome back." Her voice rang out enthusiastically, with no hint of surprised alarm, something Bet had learned to listen for when she came home unexpectedly.

Norah was wearing a draped violet poncho with a huge cowl collar that half hid her lower face. She swept it off with a single gesture at the door, shook it lightly and then came back to the office. Underneath she had on cotton pants strung loosely around her narrow hips, and a purple turtleneck that clingingly emphasized her large round breasts. She would put on a printed smock in a moment to hide them again. Norah was self-conscious about her breasts, Bet recalled once again, as they crushed briefly into her chest in a hug.

"Tell me all about your trip," Norah said, fluffing out her hair. She had masses of it, frizzy and brown, sometimes braided into cornrows, sometimes kept away from her face by pins and barrettes. Today she had on a wide plastic purple band, the kind they used to wear in grade school, that kept it out of her eyes and made it flare like a halo behind.

"I met a woman," Bet said, and stopped. She hadn't meant to mention Kelly at all. "Actually I met several." She told Norah about Judy Journeywomon as they waited for the coffee to drip through. Norah laughed as Bet had known she would. They'd always shared a sense of the absurdity of people—other people anyway.

"She'll probably turn out to be one of the major thinkers of the age," Norah said.

"You couldn't help feeling a little sorry for her," Bet said. "It's obvious she's very much in love with Mary Anne—and that Mary Anne's just tolerating her until someone more interesting turns up." She broke off. She wasn't going to talk about Mary Anne; or rather, she was, at some point, but differently.

"So who was this woman you met?" Norah asked, taking the carton of half-and-half from the refrigerator and sniffing it.

Bet started to clear off the desk, to look through the mail Norah had saved for her. "Oh, just a woman who was around. She boards her horses there, she's teaching Tam to ride."

"That's all?" Norah said, standing behind Bet and massaging her shoulders in the old way. The tips of her breasts rubbed against Bet's back, teasingly.

"That's enough," said Bet, jerking away. "My shoulders aren't sore, for one thing."

"You feel quite tight," said Norah. "Uptight, I should say."

"It's always this way," Bet burst out. "You have lovers, you don't care about me, but as soon as I even mention someone else, you're all over me."

"Well, excuse me," said Norah stiffly. "I thought we were still friends."

"We are friends, goddamnit. I just don't want you to touch me anymore, okay?"

"No problem," said Norah, pulling her smock out of the closet.

They moved around in silence for five minutes, getting the store ready to open at ten.

Suddenly Norah turned and said, "You really don't want me to touch you? Ever again?"

"I don't want you to tease me. We have to have boundaries now."

"But why those particular boundaries?"

"Because that part of us being together is over, you've said so yourself, you're the one who moved out."

"What if I said I thought it might not be permanent?"

"Then I'd think you probably had a fight with Eleanor last night and that you were feeling vulnerable."

"We didn't have a fight. I'm just not sure sometimes, that's all."

"Norah, it's been years now that this kind of crap has been going on. You falling in and out of love and making me go through it with you. We decided this time, *you* decided, that this was it. It's going to be hard enough to keep working together. It has to be purely businesslike, that's all."

"But it's so hard. I still love you, Bet."

"Then we'd better talk about breaking up the business."

"Why are you being this way this morning? Friday night when you called you really wanted to talk."

"What I wanted was to kill you. *Why* didn't you tell me about Mary Anne?"

The old secretive look came into Norah's eyes. "It was nothing, it was years ago."

"Two years."

"Years," Norah repeated. "And anyway, you said you didn't want to know things like that."

"But I still thought I knew—about all of them."

"Well, you didn't," said Norah stubbornly, but her shoulders slumped a little and she reached out a hand to Bet. Bet almost took it, stopped. It was covered with rings, bracelets clinked at the wrist.

"And this jewelry, all this goddamned jewelry," she snapped and turned away. "It makes me sick."

For the ring she had given Norah ten years ago was no longer there.

It was just before closing, while Bet was in the office, working on the books, that Norah called, "Bet, there's someone here for you."

Bet poked her head around the corner without getting up.

It was Kelly. In heavy boots, Levis and black leather jacket, holding a helmet. Her wiry brush of hair lay unbecomingly flat on her head and the crooked tooth in her awkward smile made her look like an inept pirate, especially next to Norah with her neat printed smock and delicate face. Bet was glad then she hadn't said anything more to Norah about Kelly, hadn't said, of all things, that she'd been attracted to the woman.

She introduced them, talking quickly and avoiding both their eyes. Norah retired to the office where she could, of course, hear everything.

"I thought you lived in Anacortes," Bet said in a low voice.

"We get off at three. I came down to take you out to dinner."

"Oh, well . . ." Bet stumbled nervously. "Sure , I guess . . . there's a place across the street, a Greek place. You like Greek food?"

"Whatever you like." Kelly shrugged to show it didn't matter to her, then gave Bet an intensely beseeching look. "Whatever you like, lover."

Bet ignored her, went back to the office and got her jacket. For all that she'd been interested in Kelly, all that she wanted now was to get her out of the store.

"See you tomorrow," she said to Norah, without meeting her eyes.

"Of course," said Norah coolly. "Why wouldn't you?"

"That your partner?" Kelly asked as they came outside. It was dark and chilly and misting a little. Bet pulled up her jacket collar. It was an hour and a half from Anacortes, at least; was Kelly planning to drive back tonight or did she think she was staying?

She certainly was not.

"Business partner, ex-lover," she said.

"She's pretty," Kelly said, as if puzzled. "How long were you together?"

"Ten years, something like that."

They crossed to the Greek restaurant and were seated in an alcove raining ferns. Bet found it difficult to speak for embarrassment. Was it Kelly's leather jacket, her slow, stilted walk with its cocky swagger, the way she held her shoulders, far back; the way she carried her helmet, close to her chest? She looked wrong here, exaggerated in a way she hadn't on the farm; she was out of place, in the restaurant as well as in Bet's life.

"What are you going to have?" Kelly asked, looking at the menu. Droplets of water still clung to her thin, reddened skin, but her hair was starting to spring up again.

"Their moussaka's always tolerable. I guess I'll have that." Bet closed her menu and smiled purposefully at Kelly, determined to be normal, to be cheerful. "You left pretty suddenly yesterday."

Kelly closed her menu too. "I had to get back home, finish up a few things before Monday."

"Are you always that impulsive?"

"Always. I'm down here, aren't I?" She smiled and looked intimately at Bet. "Just had the urge to see you again, baby."

Bet didn't say anything. From the corner of her eye she saw Norah come out of the storefront and lock the door. A wave of longing traveled through her. Once they'd gone home together, something that was as unthinking then as it was unthinkable now. Gone home to make dinner, to spend the evening together or apart, Bet reading, Norah studying Japanese or looking at art books while she listened to jazz on her headphone. Tonight Norah, wrapped in her violet poncho with the cowl, was getting into her car and probably going over to Eleanor's.

The waitress came over. "What can I get you?"

Bet opened her mouth. "Bet will have the moussaka," Kelly said formally. "And I'll have the chicken. And two glasses of retsina, please."

The waitress gave Bet a curious glance as she picked up the menus. Bet closed her mouth and flushed slightly.

"Tell me about your business," said Kelly. "It's much more elegant than I imagined. I thought you just sold futons."

She probably wasn't thinking, Bet decided. She sipped at her water. "It was Norah's idea originally. We made the first ones in a little house we lived in, where you could barely turn around. Neither of us knew how to sew, we'd borrowed a sewing machine from our landlady. Norah actually got fairly proficient. I could do a straight seam by the end, but I was better with the stuffing. We didn't have a store then; we used to sell them through advertising and on consignment at different alternative stores. I remember they were pretty rough and lumpy in those days . . . ."

This was the one subject Bet could talk about with any fluency these days; in this hard time the business still remained a topic she was master of, a rote lesson she could remember and expound on automatically. But the retsina came and Kelly clinked glasses with Bet, saying, "Do you know how quickly you talk when you're nervous, lover?"

Irritated, Bet said, "What about you? Mary Anne said you work at Texaco."

"I'm a welder. I'm good at it. I like it all right and it pays well. The men are total assholes, of course, but they leave me alone. I've got a house in Anacortes that I'm fixing up and it helps to have regular paychecks. My real interest is horses and art and opera and oh, a million things." She paused and drank, very aware of herself, of the impression she was trying to make. Bet almost laughed, but in the gesture of Kelly raising her glass Bet saw her again the way she had out by the pasture: head tilted, shoulders back, eyes alive, seeing the world.

"I asked Mary Anne if you were a dangerous woman and she said yes," Bet said on impulse, and did laugh.

But Kelly didn't. "Dangerous?" she said. "I'm not dangerous."

"Aren't you?" Bet tried again, smiling to show it was a joke.

"No."

A strained silence fell, just as the waitress brought their plates. I'm not going to get involved with her and I'm glad, Bet thought. She's too moody, she takes everything the wrong way. A feeling of dislike, even hostility, towards Kelly rose up in her, mixed with something else. Longing.

"I feel misunderstood," said Kelly, when the waitress had gone. "I'm a simple woman, impulsive perhaps, but nothing like—dangerous. I don't want you to be afraid of me."

"I'm not *afraid* of you, for goodness sake," Bet said impatiently. "I don't know you. I hadn't even met you when I said that to Mary Anne." She willed herself to smile, to soften her tone. "How could I be afraid of you?"

Kelly seemed to cheer up. She began to eat. "I want so much for you to know me. The way I know myself. Intimately."

Once again Bet drew back. "But you live in Anacortes," was all she could think to say.

"Why don't you move to Anacortes?"

"What?"

"Or I could move to Seattle," Kelly said seriously. "Though I don't know. I don't really like Seattle that much. I need a lot of room and I like my house, living in a house."

"I like my apartment too," said Bet, determined to treat it as a joke. "I'm happy here. In Seattle."

"You could visit me in Anacortes. I'd like for you to see my house. It's an old one, with a couple of bedrooms and lots of wood—wood floors, wood trim, wood paneling. I spent a whole year sanding once, after I broke up with someone. I was so lonely." She looked away from Bet. "Actually, that was this year."

"I'm sorry," said Bet.

They ate in silence for a while. The waitress came and took their plates and there was nothing more they could occupy themselves with. Bet excused herself for the restroom.

When she returned Kelly already had her black leather jacket on. "Shall we go?" Kelly asked.

"Fine. They can give us the check at the register."

"I've already paid it."

Bet pulled out her wallet. "How much was my share?"

"No," said Kelly, agitated. "I came down to take you out to dinner." She refused to take the ten dollar bill Bet held out, that Bet irritably put away again.

They went outside. It had stopped raining. Bet was determined not to ask Kelly to her house; still, it seemed suddenly abrupt to be saying good-bye. There had been something between them at Mary Anne's farm; it was only here that they were on the wrong footing.

"Shall I take you out for coffee and dessert?" Bet offered, in spite of herself.

Kelly nodded and took her arm. A shiver ran through Bet. Aversion? Compassion? The woman seemed so lost, so muddled, so pathetic in her little rituals of courtship. She doesn't have any friends, she's just lonely, Bet told herself. But the shiver she'd felt came from more than pity.

"Wouldn't you rather we took my car?" Bet asked, when she saw they were standing in front of Kelly's black Triumph.

"You're scared, aren't you?" Kelly suddenly swung on to the back of her motorcycle and began to put on her helmet, showing her pirate smile.

"No, of course not." Why was everything with her a tease, a fight, and why did Bet instantly rise to it, every time?

She got on behind Kelly, put her arms loosely around her waist, then more tightly as they started off. The cold November night whipped around them; the mist was settling in again. The street lights were bowls of pale gold above them. Bet clung as they rounded a corner, feeling the heat in her thighs, in her stomach. Enjoy it, she told herself, trying to be cynical. Who knows when you'll be this close to a woman again?

They arrived at the espresso cafe, parked and dismounted. Bet half expected Kelly to make a suggestive remark about the ride, but Kelly was meek and distracted, following Bet inside, putting up no protest when Bet paid for cappuccinos and two slices of hazelnut torte.

She seemed unaware of her surroundings. The minute they were seated she leaned forward and said to Bet, "I want to live with you. Can't you come back to Anacortes with me tonight and see my place? I know you'd like it."

"Are you completely crazy?" Bet whispered angrily,

even though the cafe wasn't full and no one was paying attention to them. "I don't understand you. I just met you two days ago. I've hardly talked to you. I don't even know if I like you. You turn up out of nowhere and want me to live with you. It's incredible."

Kelly didn't look surprised at Bet's outburst. "Haven't you ever acted on your feelings? I mean, put aside caution for a minute?"

"Rarely."

"What sign are you?"

In spite of herself Bet began to laugh. "Virgo. But I don't believe any of that stuff."

"I should have known," said Kelly. "You know—I thought about calling you up today and asking you if you wanted to have dinner, but I thought you'd probably say no. But I thought if I came, that I could overcome your caution, sweep you off your feet. Besides, I wanted to see your store, your house, everything. I'm Aries," she added glumly. "We'll never get along."

"But I don't believe any of that stuff."

"That doesn't matter, I do." Kelly contemplated her. "You're so beautiful, baby."

"I'd really like to go now," Bet said.

They did. This time Bet kept such a loose grip on Kelly's waist that she almost fell off.

"That's my car," she said, when they were back in front of the store. She jumped off and started towards it.

Kelly didn't turn off her engine. "Would you mind if I wrote you?"

Bet wished she could laugh, that they could both laugh at the absurdity of the situation. "I really don't care," she said without looking around.

"Good night, lover."

"Good-bye." Bet got into her car, but Kelly didn't move off. *Is she going to follow me home or what?* Bet didn't start the engine, but then she thought Kelly might wonder if there was something wrong with the car. She turned the key in the ignition and waved at Kelly. She was annoyed, and felt foolish.

Finally Kelly roared off with a brief wave.

"Lover," said Bet, and groaned.

◆*4*◆

THE MESSAGES CAME EVERY DAY. SOMETIMES THERE WERE more than one. They came on postcards of Marilyn Monroe, inside cheery all-purpose cards illustrated with teddy bears or cats; they came scrawled on notebook paper, typed on expensive stationery, coyly written on the backs of envelopes that had nothing inside.

Bet—
I'm no adventurer, though I love adventures. So much I didn't tell you, was shy about telling. Will I get another chance?

k.

thinking of you bet loving the memory of your arms around my waist

love k.a.

Bet (Elizabeth, Betty, Lisa, Liza, Eliza, Liz?)
I felt it as soon as I saw you. It frightened me terribly.
You were standing at the fence in that beautiful light.
Later, at dinner, in Mary Anne's kitchen, I just wanted to
touch you. Had to leave that morning, just to get my feel-
ings straight (no not straight, never straight!). I know it
was stupid to turn up like that at your shop (futons,
what strange things . . .) but forgive me. I don't want
you to think I'm unreliable. Impetuous perhaps, but not
a flake. I'm a serious woman, very serious about you.

My love always,
Kelly

B.—
Was out visiting my horses this weekend. I like Mary
Anne, don't you? She's so warm and practical with her
cows and chickens. Tam is wonderful, reminding me of
myself at that age. I think she'll be a great help in train-
ing young Glory. There's a tremendous amount of work
involved in training a filly and some of it needs to be
done daily. It's terrible to be at work all day and think of
all the important things I could be doing . . . Let's go to
the island together sometime . . .

Your loving Kelly

"Ever hear anything more from that Kelly person?"
Norah asked after a week or so had gone by.

"No," said Bet.

Bet read the letters through once, while walking up the
stairs to her apartment after work, then threw them into

a desk drawer without even putting them back in their envelopes. Sometimes, if she were angry coming home, angry at Norah, angry at being alone, she would throw the letters into the drawer without even opening them.

She was always restless these days, yet she didn't want to see friends. They always asked about Norah, were always so sympathetic. If they were friends who'd known about Norah's infidelities over the years they were eager now to say that the breakup was for the best, that Bet was better off on her own, that they'd never thought it would last as long as it did. If they were friends who hadn't known of Norah's affairs, they were shocked that a relationship of ten years, such a *stable, working* relationship could go under. Wasn't the conflict stage past by then, wasn't everything that could be worked out, worked out? These friends blamed it all on Eleanor.

Norah was supposedly a friend now, could have helped Bet in her loneliness and despair, but they never did the things that friends should do together and for each other: go out for a movie, or for dinner, have a real heart-to-heart, comfort each other, and promise that better times were coming.

Bet came home after work to the apartment they'd spent a year fixing up. It was the entire top of a wooden house on Phinney Ridge. Airy and light, with a view of the Ship Canal and the Olympic mountains; wooden floor and a big, old-fashioned kitchen, two bedrooms—all of it bare now, all of it looking as if a robbery had taken place.

She came home every night, ate crackers and cheese and read.

She kept reading about the Second World War, the trivial and everyday experiences of going without, of making preparations, of carrying on. In Britain they had administered an experiment called Mass Observation, where dozens of ordinary people kept diaries of their lives during the war. Bet stuck with Britain for quite a while because, while constantly threatened, they were never actually invaded. They adjusted to degrees of deprivation, adjusted and adjusted, rarely complaining seriously, enjoying themselves in small ways, trying to see the bigger picture, putting hope in the fact that England had always won in the end. The discomforts they suffered on the home front weren't the ones you might expect. It was simply ordinary life carried on under adverse and peculiar conditions. Like the blackout, for instance . . . .

Most people had to spend five minutes every evening blacking out their homes. If they left a chink visible from the streets, an impertinent air raid warden or policeman would be knocking at their door, or ringing the bell with its new touch of luminous paint. There was an understandable tendency to neglect skylights and back windows. Having struggled with drawing pins and thick paper, or with heavy black curtains, citizens might contemplate going out after dinner—and then reject the idea and settle down for a long read and an early night . . . .

For to make one's way from back street or suburb to the city centre was a prospect fraught with depression and even danger. In September of 1939 the total of people killed in road accidents increased by nearly one hundred per cent. This excluded others who walked into canals, fell down steps, plunged through glass roofs and toppled from railway platforms.

But gradually Bet began to move over to the Continent, to the occupied countries, the punished countries, where it wasn't just a matter of blackouts and black markets, but of no heat in winter and forced labor in German factories, and bread made of lupine seeds, chestnuts and sawdust, five ounces a day. The Germans were everywhere, shooting people, taking them away, taking all the best of everything for themselves.

The people console one another by saying, "Why get worked up about the problem of housing when tomorrow I mayn't have a house?"

This kind of reasoning kills all desire to possess a decent house. On the contrary, the worst kind of accommodation is sought. An out-of-the-way street is selected; all comforts, a bath, even electric lights—are avoided like the plague. Every comparatively comfortable home at once attracts the Germans, so the people never attempt to make their home convenient or beautiful. No one repairs or renovates anything. The carpets, the curtains, the pictures are kept well hidden. The worse a home can look, the more certain one feels in it.

I found an acquaintance of mine standing on a ladder pulling down the ceiling of her bathroom.

"I must give the impression that the roof might fall in at any moment," she explained, in an excess of devil-may-care humor.

The situation with Norah was worsening. The first week after the breakup had been one of tender, even exalted emotions. They would still remain close friends, no matter what. After that had come a period of uncertain politeness, exaggerated respect. They could at least keep working together, of course they could. But since Bet had gone away and come back, a bitterness had arisen on both sides; bitterness, guilt and distrust.

Sometimes Bet didn't think she could bear it. How things were now, how they might continue. Everything she'd once taken pleasure in was altered, perverted. Norah's light step moving quickly around the shop; Norah's warm, professional descriptions of the various futons, still not boring after all these years; Norah's eagerness to enter into the lives of their customers, her care to make sure they got just what they needed and wanted; her bursts of jokiness, her firmness in dealing with people on the phone; her adamant belief that theirs was the best futon store in town. Now all of Norah's behavior got on Bet's nerves, irritating and paining her from the moment she walked in the door in the morning.

She started taking an hour for lunch every day, leaving work at six-thirty on the dot, going about her tasks with a listless, sullen air. Half on purpose, to annoy Norah; half involuntarily, because she couldn't stand being there. Norah was growing snappish, veering between hurt and annoyance. She ate lunch in the store, grabbing a sandwich at her desk, stayed late every night, came in early every morning. "Well, someone's got to do the work."

There were times when Bet thought she might be starting to hate Norah. But it was as if that thought made her glad. For she surely couldn't go on loving Norah; that was more painful still.

♦ ♦ ♦

One evening, late, there was a ring at Bet's door.

"Who is it?" she called cautiously, expecting Norah. They'd nagged at each other all morning in the store, had a furious argument in front of a customer, had made up briefly, but not convincingly, just before they went home. Bet had been trying to call her on and off all evening. She didn't want to apologize, didn't expect any understanding, but all the same she wanted to hear Norah's voice, wanted that little comfort, wanted to believe they could do at least that for each other.

"Kelly."

Bet unbolted the door. The woman came in, soaking wet.

"But it's pouring outside, you rode all that way?" Bet heard her own voice, peevish and concerned. "Well, come in and have some tea anyway, take off your helmet."

Water dripped from Kelly's black leather jacket. Her face was red with pale frozen splotches and glistened with rain. "Have you got a towel?" She was uneasy but debonair. "I hadn't heard from you. I just wondered how you were. Have you been getting my letters?" She followed Bet into the bathroom for a towel and then into the kitchen. "Can't I at least give you a hug when I get dried off?"

"No!" Bet was surprised at her own vehemence. "And you can stop writing me letters and pursuing me like this! I don't like it!"

"Why not?" Kelly asked, mopping her face.

"Because! Because that's not the way I get to know people, that's why."

"You said I could write to you."

"I didn't expect a whole barrage of letters." Bet set the kettle on the stove, hard enough that water splashed from the spout. "I'm sorry, Kelly, but it just won't work. It's too strange. This isn't the right time in my life."

And then she burst into tears.

Very tenderly Kelly gathered her in her arms. She didn't say a word, but led Bet back to the living room, to the sofa.

After a moment she said, "Bet," and lifted Bet's face to kiss it.

"No," said Bet and continued to cry. But Kelly took her face in her hands and smoothed it and dried it and kissed her all around her eyes and temples, on her nose, her cheeks, her chin. Then she brushed Bet's mouth open with her chapped lips and went inside with her tongue.

And something in Bet resisted and something said yes. Her head was hot and aching and she couldn't think; there was something suffocating in the room, as if the furnace were turned on high, as if she were feverishly ill.

She found herself kissing Kelly back and putting her hands under the wet jacket, under the sweater and shirt and long underwear to feel Kelly's skin. Kelly cupped Bet's breasts; she pulled up Bet's tee-shirt so that the breasts were visible and began to kiss them.

Kelly was wearing so many more clothes; somehow Bet couldn't get further than the small of Kelly's back. Bet felt the skin there thin and hot, but the Levis were tightly belted and stiff as wet bark.

Bet was only wearing a tee-shirt and drawstring cotton pants. Kelly easily untied and slipped the pants down, along with the bikini underwear.

They were lying on the sofa, Kelly fully dressed; Bet with her legs apart now, exposed. Kelly was kissing her breasts, her stomach, lightly rubbing a finger up and down Bet's wet and swollen clitoris. Bet heard panting; it was her own voice, like some sad animal thing in a cage, moaning to get out. She had her eyes half shut; the room closed in around her, hot and furtive and crushing. For a moment she resisted, like a flame flaring up desperately from the ashes, then she suddenly gave in, gave over completely, stopped trying to unbuckle Kelly's obstinate belt, and let herself come, no, not let herself, had to, had to. She could hear, as if from the ceiling above, Kelly murmuring, "Oh baby, you really want it, don't you?"

And she did want it, because she had gone a very long time without it.

When the last flutter had died away she was still shaky and her head swam. She reached again for Kelly's belt buckle, but laughing, Kelly sat up and drew a line down Bet's stomach. She almost crowed.

"I knew I'd love to make love to you."

"But," said Bet, sitting up too. "Don't you want . . . ?"

Kelly didn't seem to hear the question. She put her wet leather arm around Bet on the sofa. "If you only knew how much I've been longing for you this past week. I'm so glad I decided to come down tonight."

Kelly suddenly jumped up from the sofa, full of energy, and walked around. "So this is where you live. This is really where Bet lives and cooks and reads and thinks and sleeps. It's so important," she turned to Bet, smiling, "to know where a person lives."

"It's empty now," said Bet, still drained and uneasy. "Norah took a lot of stuff with her."

"Yes," said Kelly. "Norah." She looked disturbed a moment, then spread her arms earnestly. "But now, you see, you have a chance to make it really yours . . . or even to move."

Bet's head throbbed so she could hardly think. The atmosphere in the room was thick and hot and weary. What had happened to make her lose her defenses? What was going to happen? Would Kelly expect to sleep here? A sudden loathing for this coltish woman rose up in Bet. Kelly hadn't taken off her fucking jacket and now she was striding around the apartment, Bet and Norah's, as if she owned it.

You'll have to go, was what Bet meant to say, but it came out, "We have to get out of here."

Bet put on her sweater and a rain slicker and took her boots out of the closet. "Come on," she said, half brusque, half listless. "We'll go have some tea or coffee somewhere."

It was about eleven-thirty. They ended up at a Denny's restaurant. They'd disagreed about whether to use the motorcycle or Bet's car. It wasn't raining anymore and Kelly wanted to feel the black night air on her skin, she said. Bet answered, fine, but she was taking her car. In the end Kelly followed her to Denny's on the motorcycle, waving to her at every red light, laughing.

When Kelly was happy she displayed a sportive, almost childish sensibility; it contrasted oddly with her general air of gravity.

At Denny's Kelly would not sit across from Bet in the booth; she sat right next to her, wanted to share the menu, to hold it together. Bet's skin crawled.

"What are you going to have?" Kelly asked as she saw the waitress approaching.

"Goddamnit," Bet almost hissed. "I don't want you ordering for me. I can tell her myself."

"Just a glass of milk," she said to the waitress, flushing at how the woman stared at Kelly.

"I'll have coffee," Kelly said, low and dignified.

"And don't try and pay for me either," said Bet aggressively.

Kelly said nothing; she looked pained.

The waitress came back with their order. Bet decided to act as if nothing had happened. "You know," she said conversationally, "I don't really know much about you, except what you told us at dinner the other night. I mean, I don't even know how you ended up in Anacortes from New York."

"Bet," said Kelly quietly. "What's wrong?"

"Nothing's wrong, goddamnit. I'd just like to know a little about you!"

Kelly sighed, said nothing, drank her coffee. "I'm a simple person, with a complicated past. I'm impulsive, I've told you that. I like women very much." She looked meaningfully at Bet and touched her thigh. "I like you very much. I could even say I love you."

Bet felt they were being stared at by everyone in Denny's. She was horribly conscious of Kelly's black leather jacket and short, flattened-down hair. Why had she ever suggested that they come here? Didn't Kelly have any sense of what was okay and not okay, of how you were supposed to act in public?

"I'm exhausted," Bet said. "I have to go home and get some sleep. Alone," she emphasized and took out her wallet.

Out in the parking lot Kelly seemed suddenly jubilant. "What a beautiful night to ride home in."

Bet felt guilty. "You know, you could sleep on my sofa . . . ."

"The ride would be hell in the morning. Right now I'm bursting with energy. But you're going to have to move to Anacortes sooner or later—you know that, don't you, lover?"

Bet didn't even bother to reply. This woman is crazy, she thought. Yet she found herself kissing Kelly swiftly and with some strangling emotion.

"I love you," said Kelly softly, and then very loudly, "I'm desperately in love with you."

Bet hurriedly disengaged herself, got into her car and drove off quickly, hoping Kelly wouldn't follow her. As she pulled up to her apartment it began to rain again.

She's sure to come back, Bet thought. Can I pretend I'm not home? Should I go to Sylvia's? But it's dangerous driving at night in the rain, she'll kill herself.

Bet went upstairs and got into bed. Her head ached badly but her body was soft and relaxed. She fell asleep still waiting for a knock.

·5·

NOVEMBER DREW IN, DRESSED IN WIDOW'S WEEDS. OUTSIDE
Bet's bedroom window the Ship Canal was a muted streak
of steely gray, lined with barren poplars, branches raised,
imploring, to the sky.

Surrounded by books on the occupation of France, Bet
started a rambling, rather disjointed letter to Kelly.

Dear Kelly,
You said you wanted to know me, but I'm not sure if
you really do. You say you're in love with me—you don't
know a single thing about me. I'm not someone you can
push around, fantasize about, make love to. It's not that
I don't find you attractive—though maybe disturbing is
a better word. For someone like me, who passes, your
queerness is a challenge. If only because it makes me so
uncomfortable. In a peculiar way I feel proud of you,
even when I'm embarrassed. But that doesn't mean I like

the way you're going about any of this. I don't trust it, it's
completely contrary to my sense of how . . .

Bet sat there trying to go on. It was true: No one had
ever pursued her before. In high school she'd had a boyfriend or two, and then there'd been Adam, Mr. Ong's
nephew who worked afternoons in the warehouse. He
was studying psychology at UCLA; they used to go to the
movies sometimes, and once they slept together, before
he got engaged. But none of those boys or men had been
desperate to be with her. The thought was ridiculous.
They were more like friends.

And with Norah, it hadn't been a matter of pursuing,
well, maybe a little bit—on each side though. Norah had
still been involved with Daniel, at the end of the relationship, but still involved.

They'd gone for a picnic at Discovery Park, she and
Norah, and afterwards for a long walk on the bluffs. It was
August. The long grass was high yellow, crackling under
their feet, parting with a swoosh on some of the less traveled paths. The sun burnt down, they both had tanktops
on, and shorts. The grasses stung beautifully. Norah said
some part of her had always been attracted to women.
They were walking single-file on the narrow path, Norah
first. Her frizzy hair was in a ponytail, and tendrils sworled
wetly on the nape of her tender neck; there was a V of
dampness on the tanktop between her shoulderblades. I
know what you mean, Bet said. Then they reached the
edge of the bluff, the grass parted and they were on the
crumbly edge looking down. Norah turned and let loose
her hair. There was the smell of dry grass, salt wind,

sweat; and their mouths were cool, their tongues like two bodies naked against each other.

Bet gave up on her letter to Kelly and wrote a stiff post-card instead:

Dear Kelly,
I'd appreciate it if you didn't call or write anymore. I'm extremely busy at the moment, and I don't think we have much in common.

Sincerely,
Bet

Sylvia called. She had been Norah and Bet's landlady during their first five years together.

"I haven't seen you for ages. Why don't you and Norah come around for Thanksgiving? Or are you going to Norah's folks?"

"Norah and I have broken up. I thought everyone knew."

Even Bet's casual tone could not make it seem less momentous than it was; both Sylvia and Bet felt it.

"I'm sorry to hear that, Bet," Sylvia said finally. "Is it recent?"

"A few weeks, maybe a month." The farther away it got perhaps the easier it would be to say. Six months ago, a year ago, two years—yes, that put it safely in the past.

"Then *you* come along. I'd love to see you."

"I'm not feeling very sociable these days."

Sylvia paused and Bet could see her clearly. Bristly gray hair cut square around a plain face, round glasses with plastic frames, a dimple in her chin. She'd be fifty soon.

"Do you mind my asking—what caused all this?"

"She's seeing someone else, a woman called Eleanor."

"And it's serious?" By which Sylvia probably meant, more serious than some of the others.

"Let's just say I took it more seriously. And so did Norah."

"Yes," said Sylvia, still trying to absorb the news. After a moment she said, "You know, I think of Norah as a very curious woman. Not curious=odd, but curious=investigative. You and she got involved when you were both just coming out. She never had a chance to experiment."

"She had plenty of chances to experiment when we were living together. That's all she did, experiment."

"But you were still living together."

"Well, I never had a chance to experiment either. I never wanted to. But I never said, no, Norah, you can't see anyone else. I let her do what she wanted for years, didn't I? It's just that I finally got sick of it."

"So it was your decision then?"

"No, it was . . . mutual."

"But Norah's enjoying herself and you're not, is that it?"

Bet couldn't stand Sylvia's matter-of-factness sometimes. "I'm seeing someone too," she felt pressed to say, just so Sylvia wouldn't think she was moping.

"Oh? Well, bring her along with you to dinner."

"I can't," said Bet. "She lives in Anacortes. She has—she has horses, she can't leave them."

Sylvia's laugh boomed. "She sounds intriguing."

"She is," Bet said glumly. "But I'm sorry I can't come to dinner. I'll call you sometime though, okay?"

"Don't sink out of sight, woman," said Sylvia. "I miss you, you know."

◆ ◆ ◆

In spite of herself, Bet was waiting for Norah to ask her to dinner at her parents'. But Norah didn't ask her. How could she ask her, they were hardly speaking. Eleanor came by almost every evening after work now. Sometimes she waited in her car outside, sometimes she stopped in. She never took off her expensive trenchcoat and never said anything to Bet beyond, "Hi, how are you?" If anyone got asked to Thanksgiving dinner at the Goldman house in Portland, it was clearly going to be Eleanor. It wasn't fair. Even though she and Norah used to groan when it was time for a holiday and even though Norah swore she couldn't sit through another dinner where Bet got passed off as her business partner to her grandmother and the more distant relatives and as a housemate and close friend to nearer relations, and even though they had to sit through awkward congratulations on their success from Aunt Helene ("These two little girls really know how to work, you've got to hand it to them!") and heavy-handed advice from Uncle Mort and Norah's father ("Get a good lawyer, that's all you need," and "Start putting that money to use, diversify."), Bet still loved holidays at the Goldman house. She loved the talk, the music, the food, even the inevitable quarreling that had to be smoothed over by Mrs. Goldman. It was so different from her own childhood home. Holidays had been celebrated there in front of the television, watching specials. Bet's grandmother was the only relative who came, and all she did was complain. The other relatives were lost or dead, and Bet's parents weren't the type to invite friends over.

Even though the Goldmans didn't particularly like Norah being a lesbian, they had accepted Bet; sometimes she'd believed they really liked her. Mrs. Goldman always made a fuss over her, kept her securely under her wing during the family uproars. "You're such a nice quiet thing, Bet, sometimes I forget you're here."

"They still treat me like a goddamn teenager," Norah had raged. "And you too. Can't they get it into their heads that we're grown women now? We have lives of our own. We're *adults*."

Was it because Bet had never really felt like a child growing up that she relished fitting into a family as a younger member? Being fussed over a little, yes, she'd always secretly liked that.The Goldmans wouldn't be able to treat Eleanor like a teenager though, not the way she dressed and acted. But maybe they'd like her. Maybe they'd think that if Bet had to go, it was better that Norah got herself an upwardly mobile girlfriend. Somebody who could order in a restaurant and knew a growth stock when she saw one.

Probably they wouldn't miss Bet at all.

Kelly called, jocularly wistful. "Why don't you come up for Thanksgiving, Bet? We could build a fire in the fireplace, have turkey with stuffing, we could cook it together. I have a lot of new records I'd like you to hear. Do you like opera—Marilyn Horne and Leontyne Price?"

"Didn't you get my card?"

"I don't understand what you're so nervous about. You treat me like I'm going to do something awful to you. What could I do? I'm perfectly harmless. I only want to make you happy, that's all I want."

"Well, I can't go up to Anacortes. I'm going to Portland with Norah. We do that every year. It's a tradition."

Kelly didn't say anything. Bet wondered if Kelly knew she was lying. "Why don't you ask some other people? You must have friends in Anacortes."

"I have a lot of friends," said Kelly, subdued. "Just not many in Anacortes. My friends are all in New York and the Bay Area. I've got one friend, she's a jazz singer who usually lives in San Francisco, but she's in Japan at the moment. A lot of my friends travel quite frequently. Another is in Amsterdam right now."

Bet stopped a sigh of irritation. It was sad really, Kelly's constant desire to impress.

"Bet, it would be so nice," Kelly wheedled. "I know you'd like it here. I really want to see you, maybe I could come down instead."

"But I told you I'm going to Portland!" Bet heard the desperation in her voice. "Because I always go to Portland!"

She went to Sylvia's that Thanksgiving. Norah and Eleanor went to Portland.

In the backyard of Sylvia's old house on Queen Anne Hill was the cottage where Norah and Bet had lived for more than five years. Every time Bet went back she recalled how hard it had been to move away from Sylvia's. Yes, the little house was too small, you could see that clearly now; there was only one room, a loft and a tiny kitchen and bath. More than three people made the space seem crowded.

Norah had wanted to leave long before Bet had. "Change can be a *good* thing, Bet. Have you forgotten there may be other nice places to live in the world? This is like playing house in a shoebox."

But Bet could still remember the excitement she'd felt when she'd first seen the little cottage, covered with climbing yellow roses, surrounded by fruit trees. It had been summer then, lush and fragrant. After four months of being lovers they were going to move in together. If they hadn't been so giddily happy they would have almost felt solemn about the event. For it meant they were serious. They were real lesbians now.

And having Sylvia as their landlady—they couldn't believe their luck. A dyke too—no hiding, no pretending. They were in and out of her house a dozen times a day. They used her washing machine, asked her advice, ate her food.

"We were like her goddamn children," Norah said afterwards.

Sylvia had worked, as she still did, at the phone company, at a modest job in personnel. During the evenings and on weekends she ran her own upholstery business. Sylvia had helped Norah and Bet with their first futons, had loaned them money to get the business started, had supported them in all their efforts.

"We owe her a lot," Bet was always reminding Norah.

"We owe her so much we're never going to get free of her if we don't get away now."

They'd moved to Phinney Ridge, to be close to the new storefront; it was from that time that Bet usually dated the change in Norah. She was restless, she wanted to live differently; she wanted to try new things, to travel. Although they each had a room to themselves in the new apartment, that wasn't enough. Norah wanted to go off by herself

from time to time, to Canada, to California. She wanted to
take vacations with other friends, to go on weekend sem-
inars with other people.

Other women, that is.

Sylvia gave Bet a quick neat hug when she came in and
took her coat. She smelled of cooking and, underneath,
Ivory soap.

"Come in," she said. "Everyone's here."

Everyone was Sylvia's son, his wife and their three
young children, several of Sylvia's friends and Lou and Janine, the current occupants of the cottage out back.

"Let's put your wine in the fridge," Sylvia said to Bet,
and, when they were alone, she looked Bet in the eye and
smoothed her cheek. "You could look worse."

"Thanks."

"No, really, how *are* you?"

"Functioning."

"But you're seeing someone. That's good."

"I don't know, Sylvia." Bet wandered around, looking
for things to eat. "I don't know what to think of her. I don't
trust her, I'm not sure I even like her—it's just that there's
some physical *thing* there."

"Don't touch that turkey . . . So you've slept together already?" Sylvia handed her some tortilla chips and then began to make the gravy. It was like it had always been: Bet
perched on a stool, at home in the green and blue kitchen
with the iron and copper pots, Sylvia in an ironed shirt
turned crisply up at the elbow. There were wrinkles now,
deep ones, and the hair was entirely gray, not streaked,
but Sylvia was just the same.

"Sort of."

"What do you mean, sort of?"

Bet tried to explain their late night encounter.

"Oh god," said Sylvia. "A stone butch."

"No she's not!"

"But she won't let you touch her, right?"

"Maybe it was just that one time," Bet pleaded, and then remembered herself. "Anyway, I don't *want* to touch her. I don't even want to know her."

"I see," said Sylvia, so seriously that Bet knew she was trying not to laugh. "What's the problem then? Nobody's making you be with this woman."

"I'm not with her," said Bet. "I don't even like her much, I don't think. Oh, I don't know what to think. But I'm not *with* her."

"I see," said Sylvia again, and this time she did laugh, the booming laugh that, by the end, Norah used to say drove her crazy. "It sounds like she may think otherwise."

Bet lingered after dinner, reluctant to go home. Lou and Janine had washed the dinner dishes, the grandchildren had been sleepily packed in the back seat, lingering good-byes had been exchanged among all the old friends. Now Lou and Janine and Sylvia and Bet were sitting around in the living room, just as Bet and Norah had done so many times in the past.

Bet couldn't help it; she felt jealous of Lou and Janine. They were both twenty-five; Lou was in graduate school, in urban planning. Janine was working as a legal secretary. They had been together a year, but had only just started living together.

"Isn't Sylvia just great," Lou had burbled to Bet earlier. "We feel so lucky to have found this house. It's a little small for two people, but it's so cozy."

Just wait, Bet felt like saying. In a few years one of you will start feeling it's too small, that you're spending all your time with Sylvia. One of you will start wondering why Sylvia doesn't have a steady lover, why she can't hang on to anyone, why she takes such an interest in your lives. The other will feel that Sylvia is another mother, only better because she wants you around.

But all she said was, "Yes, very cozy."

Now Sylvia poured out cups of decaf espresso.

"Oh my," she said, stretching out on the sofa and taking off her glasses. "Every Thanksgiving I swear I'll never do it again. It's exhausting to have all these people over, even though I love it. What'd you think of my friends, by the way?"

"It's always interesting," Janine said, "seeing couples who've been together for years and years."

"It makes you wonder," Lou went on, "why people choose each other, what keeps them together."

"Personally I think it's just credit card debt," said Sylvia. "What's your opinion?"

Janine laughed and looked sideways at Lou. "We don't call it butch and femme or anything like that," she said. "But we like to look at women, at other couples, and we call them apples and oranges."

Sylvia put her glasses back on to look at them. "That's novel."

Lou explained, "Every couple is made up of an apple and an orange, okay? Now, we've noticed that when a couple breaks up, the apple goes out and finds another orange, and the same with the orange. She'll only get involved with an apple. Or if she gets involved with an orange, she won't stay with her. Apples and oranges are the long-term couples."

"You don't usually find apples and oranges being friends," said Janine. "An apple would worry about her orange lover only if the orange met another apple. But oranges can be friends with oranges, that happens all the time."

Sylvia smiled, but looked thoughtful. "Why don't you just say butch and femme, if that's what you mean?"

"But don't you see, that makes us nervous," said Janine earnestly. "Whereas, if we use words like apple and orange, we take it out of the realm of judgment."

"And remove it from an historical context," added Lou.

"So what are apple's characteristics, then?" asked Bet. "What are orange's?"

"Well, like Sylvia's friends tonight. Mona's an apple and Pauline's an orange," said Janine, and Lou went on, "Jennifer is an orange and Mary's an apple."

"How can Pauline and Jennifer both be oranges?" Sylvia interrupted. "Jennifer's a femme if I ever saw one."

"I'm not sure if I understand your criteria," Bet said. "Is it the body someone's born with? Whether they're big or small or have breasts or don't? Their clothes? Haircut? Movements? Is it the work they do? Their socialization or resistance to it? What?"

Lou answered patiently, "You can't take an apple separately and an orange separately and try to characterize them. Apples and oranges go together; it's the interaction between them that's the main thing, the fact that they're attracted to each other."

"So you can't be an apple without an orange, or vice versa?" Bet wanted to know. "What if you're unattached? Are you a banana then?"

"Stop with all the fruit!" Sylvia held up two warning hands. "This is getting a little ridiculous. There are definitely women defining themselves in roles, the way they always have. It's just a question of whether you want to do it, whether it helps you live your life or just gives you a kick. Or if you're the kind who sees privilege or power attached to a style. Some people need or want roles, others don't. How about you two?"

Bet looked at Lou and Janine. One was slightly taller than the other, with a squarer jaw; the other was rounder, a bit softer. But for the most part they looked and talked surprisingly alike. They gave off an air of reinforcing wholeness that was a little uncanny.

"Noooo," said Lou finally. Janine didn't say anything.

"At one time I considered myself pretty butch," Sylvia said.

"You?" said Janine. "But you were married, had a kid . . . ."

"What does marriage have to do with it?" asked Sylvia. "That was just something to get out of the house. The kid came because I didn't know any better, though I love him now. But he mainly grew up with my sister's kids. When I ran away from my husband and started hanging out with the bar crowd, I didn't have any problem deciding who I wanted to identify with. The real queers, that's how I thought of them. The women in pants and suit jackets. Forget the dresses and the beehive hair . . . If you'd asked me then I would have said that butch was a way of being strong, of standing, of holding yourself, of looking people straight in the eye. To me it was less about sex than taking your space, taking your power, taking on other people if you had to." Sylvia sighed. "When I was a kid, in my neighborhood anyway, that's how I had to be to just get along."

Janine was still a little open-mouthed. "But you seem such a, such a . . . " she gestured around the living room, at the warm mix of fabrics and surfaces. "*Mother*," she said finally.

"Well, I had that in me too," Sylvia said. "Though I didn't realize it at first. I was a terrible mother to my kid in the beginning. I wanted to be wild and free and tough. It was only when I met Nancy, only as time went on and we got to know each other and lived with each other, that I gradually felt safe enough to show more of my self."

"What made you change?" asked Lou.

"Nancy, I guess. Or maybe I changed myself, who knows?"

There was a silence, then Bet said, "I wonder why we divide it all up, when we could have so much more, when we could have the whole thing?"

"Because people think it's sexy," said Sylvia briskly and got up to close the drapes on the dark November evening. "And in lots of ways, yes, I suppose it is."

When she got home that evening Bet tried to call Kelly, though it was late. She had a guilty feeling about the woman, about her lonelinesss—how different was it from Bet's own? She tried the next day and the next. There was never any answer.

She thought about Norah all the time, she couldn't help it. She sat there in the bare apartment for three days and read war memoirs obsessively and all the time she was thinking about Norah and Eleanor in Portland. What was so great about Eleanor, what did she have, except newness, that Bet didn't have?

What had any of them had?

She'd been too afraid to ask, and Norah had never told her.

On Sunday evening she finally reached Kelly.

"Oh hi," said Kelly casually. "How was Portland?"

"I ended up with some friends in Seattle instead." Bet was aware she sounded aggrieved rather than apologetic. "I tried to call you to invite you to eat with us," she said and almost believed it herself. "But you weren't home."

"Oh, I stopped in at Mary Anne's," Kelly said. "There were a lot of people, lots of food, singing afterwards, games. It was fun." She didn't elaborate.

"Did you give Tam more riding lessons? How's she doing?" Bet prodded. For the first time since she'd met Kelly the woman seemed untalkative.

"Sure did, she's doing fine."

There was an awkward silence. The long distance sound of the call buzzed in Bet's ears. Kelly was mad at her. Kelly had asked Bet to Thanksgiving dinner and Bet had refused. Bet hadn't treated Kelly well at all.

"I was thinking," Bet said finally. "I, umm, need to get away for a few days. I was thinking, maybe I'd come to Anacortes to visit you one weekend."

"You'd come here?" Kelly was immediately excited. "Oh, Bet, that'd be great. There's so much I want to show you. God, I can hardly believe it. Saturday morning. You'll come Saturday morning?"

Saturday morning it was then.

·6·

BET DIDN'T ARRIVE IN ANACORTES UNTIL THREE IN THE afternoon on Saturday, and that was after postponing it as long as she could. During the week she'd had serious reservations and several times on the endless drive she wished she hadn't said she was coming and intermittently she thought of turning back. The Skagit Valley was a landscape of frostbite; a cold mist seemed to isolate each weathered farmhouse as if it were white tissue paper crinkled around a faded, unimportant little object.

Even though she was driving to Kelly she kept thinking about Norah.

Monday and Tuesday Norah had been very quiet, unusually so. She'd rearranged parts of the shop and made a new display for the front window, using some ingenious rag dolls that Eleanor, who was an art collector as well as a highly paid management consultant, had found on a recent trip to Peru.

"South America doesn't exactly convey the mood of all the Asian junk we've got in here," Bet muttered.

"I don't see why we should be limited, limit ourselves to Japan and China," said Norah. "There's a big market for all sorts of imports."

"I thought we were selling futons?"

"Futons can no longer be considered just an Asian import—they're international. That's the point I'm trying to make with the window. If you have a better idea I'd be glad to hear it."

Norah adjusted some of her jewelry, which, as Bet looked at it, seemed to be South American too. More presents from Eleanor?

That had been Monday. Bet had dropped the subject of the window. Who cared, anyway, where the dolls came from? Of course it looked wonderful, as Norah's displays always did.

On Tuesday she had finally broken down and asked Norah about her long weekend. Norah had responded vaguely with, "My parents are fine. They send their love."

She hadn't asked Bet about her own Thanksgiving, other than to say, "I hope Sylvia's doing well."

Bet hadn't answered. Why tell her about the apples and the oranges; she'd probably think it was stupid. Norah had never wanted to be an ordinary fruit. When she was just coming out she'd loved Colette and the Natalie Barney crowd, and she'd still never been in a gay bar. She probably thought of herself as a pomegranate or something. Colorful, exotic, full of closed-off compartments and, when it came down to it, inedible, too many indigestible useless little pits. And Eleanor with her sports car, her travels, her designer trenchcoat was a kiwi fruit, flown in from another climate, a garnish for nouvelle cuisine. Well, they could have each other.

On Wednesday it all surfaced. After work, as they were closing up, Bet said suddenly, surprising herself, "I want out. Out of the business."

Norah had been taking off her smock. Her full round breasts were heartbreakingly visible for a moment in her silk turtleneck. Then she pulled the smock down again and turned, furious, to Bet. "Oh fine, great time to tell me, just when we're in the middle of the holiday season."

"I'm supposed to tell you when the store is packed with customers? I'm supposed to tell you when you're getting into Eleanor's stupid sports car? Or call you up in the middle of the night at her house? Come on, when do we ever see each other long enough to talk anymore? You don't know a goddamn thing about my life any longer and you don't want to. Well, I'm sick of it, I don't feel like we should be working together, I don't feel like I belong here. I want out."

"It's so convenient for you to put the blame on Eleanor, isn't it? You don't know her or anything about our relationship. You don't care either. She's just a scapegoat."

"Yeah, that's right. I'm the one with all the problems, I know, I always have been. What was wrong with me that I didn't like a triangle, for instance, that I began to be suspicious of you—"

"I've never lied to you, if that's what you're getting at."

"Why didn't you? It would have been easier than the blow by blow accounts."

"Your jealousy has corroded my life."

And so it had gone on; in the course of the next hour they told each other everything they'd been storing up over the last month. For some reason Norah still clung to the idea of the store, however, of working with Bet. Bet might be a horrible person, but Norah still wanted to work with her. It was Bet who wanted to break up the partnership. And she resolved she would.

They would get through the holiday season as best they could and in January see a lawyer. Bet would stop working December 31.

The only thing that didn't seem at issue was who should keep the business. They were both clear that it was more Norah's than Bet's, though whether it had started out that way or had evolved, was difficult to say.

There were Christmas decorations up and down Commercial Ave in Anacortes: tinsel and snow-flecked Santa Clauses, snowmen and nativity scenes. The windows of the stores were decorated with green holly leaves and curvy red holiday wishes; the glass brushed with flecks of fake snow like dandruff. The decorations still had the meager novelty of the first week in December. By the time New Year's day rolled around, they would have begun to seem intolerable.

There was little else to make the town festive. How could a woman who'd grown up in New England have settled in this rough western city? It had all the drawbacks of modern America, billboards and parking lots and every cheap chain store and restaurant invented, with none of the quaint charm of Port Townsend or Bellingham.

Bet didn't know what to imagine when it came to Kelly's house. She half thought that Kelly might be living in a trailer park. But she also wondered if Kelly might not completely surprise her, as she'd done before, and own a multi-story mansion overlooking Rosario Strait.

The reality lay somewhere between the two. The house was a modest but roomy wood frame with a big wooden porch, painted white with blue trim. It sat on the hill facing the narrow channel between Anacortes and Guemes Island and had a view of Mount Baker off to the right.

Kelly and a black cocker spaniel came around the side of the house as Bet pulled up in front. Kelly was wearing a heavy sweater and jeans, carrying an ax. Her face broke into a wide smile when she saw Bet get out of the car. Bet was touched. Kelly would never be the sort to hold a grudge. She wouldn't punish Bet for being late, wouldn't withhold like Norah.

Still, the habit of apology was unstoppable. "There was more to finish up in Seattle than I thought."

"At least you got here while it's light, that's the important thing . . . . Oh, Bet," said Kelly, and touched her arm, then embraced her. "I've been longing for this for weeks. For you to see me, where I lived."

"Well, I'm here," said Bet, stiffening a little as she always did at public displays of affection, but feeling the warmth of Kelly's body go through her with an intensity she'd almost forgotten.

"It's very important to me," said Kelly, stepping back and smiling. Then she said, with no change in tone, only happiness and excitement, "I'm not going to be here much longer. I'm moving to the island."

"You are?" said Bet, unable to think clearly. "Why?"

"You know her," said Kelly, and gave a little shout. "Mary Anne. And we're going to have a big housewarming and we want you to come."

"Oh," said Bet, and closed her mouth. She looked away from Kelly, down at the dog. "Well, that's great, congratulations . . . . Say, what about some coffee? I'm kind of tired."

"You know, I don't think I have any coffee. Life has been so crazy lately. But let's go downtown and get some. I want to show you around anyway. I know you've driven through it, but there are things only I can point out and explain. We'll take my car."

Another surprise. She'd thought Kelly only had the motorcycle. This was a nice old Saab.

Why was it that everything seemed different about Kelly now? She didn't seem dangerous and threatening; she still seemed totally unpredictable, but there was a childlike, even sweet aspect to her voice and gestures that took Bet off guard. She didn't understand it; why was Kelly so happy to see her, to have finally gotten her to Anacortes, only to tell her she was moving in with Mary Anne?

Mary Anne! But Mary Anne had never shown any interest in Kelly. She had Judy. She'd agreed that Kelly was dangerous, had made her sound like she was unreliable and a little crazy. She'd helped Bet form an opinion of Kelly as unstable and not to be trusted. And here she was letting Kelly move in.

"But what about Judy?" asked Bet, because she couldn't ask, was either too proud or too humiliated to ask, What about me?

They were waiting for the Saab to warm up. Kelly had pulled on well-worn leather gloves and a silk scarf. Her wiry hair crested above her straight profile. Outside, the black cocker had given up leaping about and had gone back to the porch, where she stared at them with hurt eyes.

"Judy's too young for Mary Anne," Kelly said. "Mary Anne needs a woman, a woman's loving."

"But what about me?" Bet burst out. "I mean, I thought we were . . . getting to know each other."

Kelly said nothing, fiddled with the radio. "Are you one of those old-fashioned types?" she asked finally, and gave Bet's knee a squeeze. Her eyes were warm and challenging.

Bet withdrew. "Yes, I am."

"But, Bet, I've known you for a month now. You've never given any indication that you wanted to get involved with me. On the contrary, you've pushed me away any chance you got." Kelly drove quickly and carelessly down the street. "I thought you'd be happy for me."

"I am happy for you," Bet said sullenly. She felt like a fool. "How did it happen?" she asked, though she didn't really want to know.

"On Thanksgiving. Oh, we'd talked about it once before. I'd told her during the fall that we ought to have an affair, and she'd just laughed. This time when I told her she agreed. God, it was a nice weekend . . . okay, now we're coming to downtown. I wish you could see it with my eyes, how much this town interests me."

Numbness had set in. It was always like this. Bet's feelings seemed to freeze over, like a pond, first just the surface, so she could still feel them moving slowly underneath, like fish in winter, then it all froze, right down to the bottom, locking everything in place before it could move around any more and cause damage.

"Anacortes was named for a woman, Anna Curtis—they changed it to sound Spanish like the rest of the area around here. Land speculators and dreamers bought up all the land; they expected this city to be the western terminus of the transcontinental railway and the link to the Orient. The city limits are huge; they platted out a little utopia here and thousands of people came. They had two banks, a school, churches, two newspapers, five wharves to accommodate all the ships that would come here and five depots for the railroad."

Kelly drove down side streets and showed Bet the few remaining buildings from that era. The railroad had never come. It went to Tacoma, then Seattle. Anacortes was left out, and then the financial bust came. By 1892 it was practically a ghost town. "Maybe that's why I like it so much," Kelly said, pulling up in front of a cafe and parking. "It had big ambitions, it was going to be the center of the universe."

Inside the cafe Kelly took off her scarf, greeted the waitress familiarly and ordered coffee and two pieces of blackberry pie for them. She seemed at home and happy, talking once again about her horses. She was thinking of letting Nutmeg foal again, now that she would be there to help and to train the foal. Glory had never really gotten the attention she deserved, but now all that would change. She was going to give up her job at Texaco. She'd become a farm hand; that life suited her best. She and Mary Anne would increase the dairy herd. What the island really needed was a bona fide dairy—pasteurizing, bottling equipment. It had had a dairy once, in the forties.

Outside the cafe, evening fell like a hat pulled over a sleeping face. It was the hour before people got off work and the streets were deserted. The decorated street lamps went on sadly. In the hardware store directly across, a snowman blinked on and off, a satellite sending signals.

Finally Bet roused herself. "I'd like to see your house and then I've got to go," she said. "I want to get home before it's too late."

For the first time Kelly looked uncertain. "I thought you were planning to stay the weekend."

"That was before I knew . . . ." Suddenly it was too much. "You planned this weekend with me and all the time you'd made the decision to move in with Mary Anne. I can't believe it." She stood up and took the check over to the cashier.

In the car Kelly seemed subdued. Bet's brief moment of self-righteous resentment had passed. She felt lonely, lonely and rejected.

Bet began to cry as they were sitting in front of the house. Outside the cocker yelped wildly at the car door.

Kelly leaned towards Bet over the stick shift and stroked her knee and thigh. Bet could barely see her in the twilight.

"Bet, why are you crying?"

"Because, because—now I'll never get a chance to know you."

The wail surprised even her. She felt desolate, sick at heart.

"Oh god, I love you," Kelly said. "Maybe I'm making the wrong choice."

"You are," Bet choked out.

Kelly was kissing her neck now, putting one gloved hand and one bare hand on Bet's breasts under her coat and sweater; she slipped her bare fingers down inside Bet's pants.

"Oh Christ, you're soaking," she said."Oh baby, let it come."

With expert fingers she nuzzled and rubbed and kneaded; at the same time she had Bet's head back and her tongue deep in Bet's mouth.

Bet felt an uncontrollable abandon. So what if they were parked on the street in front of a house in Anacortes; so what if anybody could come by? All the better. She felt waves of desire rippling down through her legs and the soles of her feet were as hot as if she were standing on live coals. It was the same as before; she was near coming from the moment Kelly touched her, but this time she held off as long as she could. Like a red message flashing on the freeway at night—SINGLE LANE, SINGLE LANE—— phrases blinked on and off in her mind: *I don't know where I am, I can't help myself, I have to, I have to* . . . and then Bet came, loudly and so violently she arched backwards in her seat.

"Let'em know it, baby," Kelly murmured in her ear, and rocked and held her as she fell, throbbing.

After a minute or two Bet realized she was cold and sticky. Kelly put on her second glove again, almost professionally.

"Shall we go inside and have some dinner?" she asked. "You'll stay the night, I hope."

"Look, I've got to talk to you," said Bet. She almost pleaded, Why don't you want to be touched? Let me touch you. Instead she said, "We need to talk about this Mary Anne thing." Her voice sounded hard and accusing.

But Kelly was too pleased with herself and the world to hear. She opened the car door and stood up, breathing deep and looking at the sky. "I bet you never see the stars in Seattle, do you?" She bent down and picked up the black cocker, who licked her hysterically all over her face.

Bet struggled out of her seat too, to stand on the other side of the car. "You'll be able to see them even better on the farm," she said snidely.

"Exactly," Kelly laughed. "Oh Bet, can you understand? I don't want to have a long distance relationship with anyone. I need to live with someone. I've been so lonely, so terribly lonely this last year." She started towards the house, putting down the dog and pretending to toss something to it without having anything in her hand. "I know you'd never want to live in Anacortes—you couldn't, with your business. And I could never live in Seattle. I don't feel comfortable there."

Bet followed her, furious. "You set up an impossible choice, me living here or you in Seattle—then you choose something entirely different. Why are you moving in with Mary Anne?"

Kelly opened the front door and the black cocker shot inside. "I like Mary Anne," she said. "We've been friends for quite a while now. And I love the idea of living with Tam too." She turned to Bet and smiled. "It's like having a daughter to raise . . . well, come on in, this is my house. Oh Bet, I'm so happy you're here!"

·7·

WHAT BET NOTICED FIRST WERE THE WEAVINGS, GOLD, TAUPE and brown, dry absorbent landscapes, one to each wall, making a different weather than the wet, wood-smoky atmosphere outside. The weavings were grand and spacious, interspersed around them, in no particular order were photographs and the kind of postcard Kelly liked to send to Bet: black and white movie stills and teddy bears.

There was a bareness to the place: a polished wood floor with a faded oriental rug, thickened by dog and cat hair; a closed off fireplace with a black Jotul stove in front, a sliding glass door without any drapes, and a long nubby ivory sofa covered with black dog hair. On one armrest a fluffy white cat made an extra pillow; a second white cat was curled up in a rocking chair. There were no books around, but there was a large screen television and an elaborate stereo and compact disc system. A few cardboard boxes were about.

"I'm just starting to pack," Kelly said, uncertain for a moment. She seemed conscious suddenly that some things about the room were not quite right and tried to excuse them. "I used to live with a woman and she took a lot of things with her when we broke up. Like you and Norah."

"How long ago was that?"

"A year—a little less. It was right after Christmas." Kelly threw herself on the sofa, dislodging the white cat. The black cocker jumped up next to her and licked her face adoringly.

"Yes, oh, little dog, yes, you love me, don't you?"

Bet turned away to the picture window. There was a porch out in back and a strip of grass, but most of the view was firs, tall and black as crows with their wings closed. In the reflection of the glass she caught a glimpse of Kelly's aquiline profile and again was strangely moved by its clean lines. She went back and sat down next to her, patting the little dog hesitantly.

"What's her name?"

"Lulu. She's been with me for a long time, years and years, haven't you, Lulu-wu-wu?"

Lulu barked and stared at Bet mistrustfully.

"I got her when I lived on the farm in Vermont. And now we're going back to the farm, aren't we, Lu?"

Bet got up and walked around, pretended to look through the compact discs. "So, what's to eat?"

Kelly bounded to her feet and showed Bet the kitchen. It had a maple table and chairs and a calico-shaded lamp hanging down over them. The appliances were all new, and the counterspace looked almost untouched.

"We put a lot of money into the kitchen," Kelly said, pouring a rattling stream of dog food from a bag into

Lulu's dish, and opening a can of tuna for the two cats
who swarmed around her feet. "Jessica loved to
cook . . . But now," Kelly opened up the freezer of the
enormous refrigerator and took out a pile of frozen
gourmet dinners. "Here we've got LeMenu Turkey Scallopine and LeMenu Chicken Breast Florentine and also one
Sweet and Sour Pork. And some Pepperidge Farm ones
too, shrimp . . . would you like shrimp?"

"That's fine."

Kelly selected Turkey Scallopine for herself and put the
others back in the freezer. She opened the lower door of
the refrigerator and investigated its cavernous spaces. "Ar-
tichoke hearts, a little jar of them, what do you know?
Want them? Or look, here's a jar of antipasto, you know,
marinated vegetables. I didn't remember these were here.
We'll have them for hors d'oeuvres." She pulled out a bottle of white wine.

"To celebrate!" She winked at Bet.

Bet watched her as she shoved the dinners in the oven
and took out a corkscrew. She realized she'd never before
seen Kelly doing anything but riding or driving or eating.
These small intimate tasks in the kitchen made her seem
more vulnerable; watching her gave Bet the same feeling
she used to have when she saw her father in the kitchen
on Mother's Day. The thought depressed her.

"Did Jessica work at Texaco too?" she asked.

"Jessica?" Kelly laughed, pouring the wine and handing
Bet a glass. "Jessica was a weaver. Those are her weavings
in the living room. She had a studio in the garage."

"They look like they're from the Southwest."

"Well, that's where I met her. We came here together.
Skoal. Cheers. To love, lover."

Bet ignored her. "I didn't know you'd ever lived in the Southwest."

"I never have. Just passing through. Jessica was hitching, trying to get away from her husband to the Northwest—she'd heard it was beautiful. So I decided to take her here."

"And you became lovers?"

"Yes, the first night, under the stars in the desert," Kelly said, drinking her wine. "She'd never had a woman make love to her before."

"You always say 'make love to,' never 'make love with,'" Bet burst out.

Kelly looked at her thoughtfully. "You'd like it to be different, wouldn't you, Bet? More equal."

Bet didn't say anything; she felt ashamed of her anger. Why was she always attacking Kelly? "It's just that, I'd like to give you pleasure too."

"I get a lot of pleasure from watching you, touching you."

There was a simplicity about Kelly that was both disconcerting and misleading. Bet said, carefully, "Whatever happened between you and Jessica?"

"It just didn't work out . . . she didn't like Anacortes. She wanted to live on one of the islands, but couldn't figure out how to get by. I got the job at Texaco because I've had experience and I'm strong. She worked for a while as a restaurant cook and then in a little crafts shop. The rain got to her, everything got to her. She went back to New Mexico."

"So she wasn't the woman you were involved with for years and years. The woman with the farm in Vermont?"

"Margo? No, that was a long time ago. Want to see some pictures?" Kelly jumped up. "I'll go get them."

They weren't in albums or scrapbooks, but in their original Kodak envelopes, dozens of envelopes in a box. Kelly opened one of them at random, ruffled through the contents, closed it; she opened another.

"Oh my god, I'd forgotten about these." Shy but not indifferent, she held out the envelope to Bet, and got up to check the frozen dinners. When she sat down again Bet was staring at a photo of Kelly in her mid-twenties, thin as a rail and with her hair slicked back, standing with her arm around an older woman in a long turquoise tunic and open-toed heels. The woman's blond hair was pulled back into a bun. She was plump, even puffy in the face, with a sour mouth and too much eye make-up.

"That was Margo."

"She was a lesbian? She looks so straight."

"She had an art gallery . . . they all dressed like that," Kelly said and shrugged. She flipped through more of the photographs. "Here we are on the farm in Vermont. That was my first horse, a registered thoroughbred, Daring Lady."

In the photograph Kelly was in jodphurs and a white shirt, with an ascot carefully tied at her throat. She seemed strikingly young and handsome, smiling in a different way from how she did now. Standing by the horse and holding the reins, was Margo, in riding costume too. Her blond hair was in a French twist.

"So you just went back and forth between the Village and Vermont and Margo paid for everything?" Bet said.

Kelly nodded. "That's how it worked for eight or nine years. I did everything for her—around the gallery, at the farm—but I didn't get paid. That would have insulted us both. We had a joint account . . . of course she kept her real money in another bank."

"What happened, how did you break up?"

"I was bored and restless. One day I just left. Actually, I joined the Army. I wanted to do something different. That's how I learned welding."

"The Army!" Bet was astonished and horrified.

"I knew you'd react like that," said Kelly, laughing. "Margo was completely beside herself. People from her circle never did things like that. She broke off contact with me. Maybe that's why I did it. I like the irrevocable."

Bet didn't say anything. The irrevocable was just what she didn't like. She picked up another photograph at random: Margo on a stone terrace, drink in hand, laughing with a group of women. She looked happier, the sour expression gone from around her mouth. "Were these friends of yours?" Bet asked.

Kelly looked at them briefly. "Yes. Donna and Jean, Merle and Connie. They were part of our little circle. Margo liked to drink with them . . . . It got to be so stifling at times. But occasionally I miss them now, wonder what it would have been like if I'd been able to stick it out. Margo and I had a good life together—it's been harder since. Though more interesting."

Bet felt they were finally getting somewhere. "So you joined the Army. And then what?"

"I had some money, I traveled around, trying to see where I might want to live. I'd been stationed in the South, in Alabama, and I knew I didn't want that. I went to San Francisco and hung out there for a couple of years, went to the Southwest and met Jessica. And here I am."

"And here you are," repeated Bet. The random, offhand manner of Kelly's summary astonished some part of herself, almost made her angry. "Here you are, moving to the island."

Kelly got up and took out the dinners. She poured them both more wine. Suddenly she had become intense.

"I need to be with my horses if I'm going to do anything with them, Bet. They need to be exercised regularly, Glory needs training. What's the point of having horses if you can't train them?"

"You could stable them nearer to Anacortes. You used to. You said you didn't want to see them too much."

Kelly ignored that. "I think Tam is going to be great with them. God, it's so exciting to see her. She reminds me of myself when I was younger—just at that age where you're turning from tomboy to baby dyke."

"Look, could we talk about something else, please? I find it extremely strange to be talking about you moving to the island, moving in with another woman, while I'm here eating dinner with you."

Kelly paused a moment. "But I have to live with a woman, it's my nature. I don't like halfway measures. And you would never want to live with me."

"How do you know? Why couldn't we?" Bet stopped herself. "No, you're right. I don't want to live with anybody right now."

"Where would I stable my horses in Seattle?" Kelly worried.

"It's always your goddamn horses," Bet said. "You never mention Mary Anne. It's always Tam and the fucking horses."

"Mary Anne and I have an understanding," Kelly said. "It's not romantic like you and me. Mary Anne and I just get along." Kelly smiled, almost impishly. "She knows when I'm bullshitting; she laughs when I'm acting crazy or when I change my mind. You're just shocked and dismayed."

Bet stolidly ate her shrimp dinner, on the verge of tears. It was true, she was not an easy person to get along with; she was impossible, a failure. Wasn't it true from Norah's many defections and betrayals, from her moving out to be with Eleanor? There was something inadequate about Bet and there always had been. Her parents had thought so, her mother especially. "You're so moody, Betty. All right, sulk in the bathroom, *I* don't care."

"Music, I forgot the music," said Kelly suddenly. "Just because we're eating frozen dinners in the kitchen doesn't mean we shouldn't have the best of the Met." She raced out and put on Leontyne Price singing Puccini. When she returned she was beatific.

"I get this vision of life sometimes," she said. "That it's so rich and there's so much to do. Opera, horses, art—I love them all. I wish I were the sort of person who could learn languages, I'd love to learn about ten—Russian and Sanskrit, Chinese, Urdu. And travel around the world and see what there is to see. That's what I loved about living in New York. Oh, there was so much to do. You could go to the opera, to the museums . . . ."

She's crazy or she's drunk, Bet thought, though she too had had her visions at times and was even moved by Kelly's. Bet drank more wine and felt very tired. Norah sometimes used to say the same sorts of things, but with Norah you had the feeling she would do them. Norah had learned Japanese. And if Norah said she wanted to go to China, she would. Norah was rooted in some practical soil that made the extraordinary ordinary. With Kelly it all seemed like bullshit, lies and longings and bullshit. If Mary Anne could laugh at it, more power to her. Bet just found it pathetic.

But suddenly Kelly cupped Bet's face in her hand and spoke to her tenderly. "You look so tired, Bet, you look so sleepy. Come and lie down."

Bet was tired, but more than that, she felt passive, will-less in some way, sucked into Kelly's world. She couldn't imagine staying, but she couldn't imagine driving back to Seattle either. She would have to have some coffee.

They went and sat on the sofa. Leontyne was singing "Si, mi chiamano Mimi" from *La Boheme*. Bet put her head on Kelly's shoulder and instantly fell asleep. Just for a few seconds, but long enough to have a vivid little dream. She and Kelly were in the desert, at the bottom of an arroyo. They were walking along the dry stream bed, looking at the stones and pebbles. "When they're wet they glisten," Kelly said and turned to look at her. "I can make them glisten," she said and Bet said, "I want you more than I've ever wanted anyone in my whole life."

She woke up at the close of the song with these words on her lips and lifted her face to find Kelly staring down at her with the same tender intensity of the dream in her eyes.

They got up without speaking and went into Kelly's bedroom. All that was there was a king-size bed and a small table with a clock radio. On the wall was a huge weaving of the Southwest, a canyon cracked open under the hot blue sky.

Kelly threw off her clothes quickly and jumped under the covers. "It's cold!"

Bet undressed more dreamily. She'd caught a glimpse of the red digits winking in the clock. It was only 7:57. The unnatural hour for going to bed, combined with the darkness and silence of the unknown place around her gave her the sense that she was acting in some erotic film, that she was not quite herself. She was conscious of Kelly looking up at her as she pulled off her sweater and folded it up, then slowly unzipped her jeans and pulled them down halfway.

Bet sat on the side of the bed to take off her boots so she could get her jeans down. As she bent over, Kelly leaned towards her and ran a finger around the elastic of Bet's bikinis. She snapped it several times, then slid her finger down into the cleft between the cheeks. Deliberately Bet bent further over and let her hands rest on the floor, and Kelly moved her finger around and up inside Bet. They both moaned at the wetness they found there. Kelly put another finger in and then another, stroking up and down, teasing and pressing gently, then more firmly. Head between her knees Bet rocked back and forth on the fingers, working them, and sounds began to come out of her mouth, half incoherent pleadings and cries of desire. Her thighs shook; tremors ran through her entire body, and when she put her own hands to her breasts the nipples were taut and electric.

Broken phrases choked her mind: want, need, please. All there was in the world was Kelly's hard-soft fingertips in her, pressing down, as if on the button in the elevator that would open doors on the seventy-eighth floor, up where there was no building anymore, only sky . . . and everything was dark and soft as she went pulsating into that new space, her physical body collapsing into something that was no longer familiar.

She came back to herself slowly; the room was black as cat fur and smelled of sex. She reached for Kelly's legs and spread the thighs. Kelly stiffened and tried to move away. Bet wouldn't let her. Still with her jeans halfway down and her boots on, she lay heavily across Kelly and put her face down through the triangle of crinkly hair to the softness underneath.

"It won't work, it's too hard," Kelly breathed, but there was an undercurrent of longing in her voice. Bet began slowly. She felt a powerful patience; she felt strong and alive, as if she could keep Kelly pressed open and lick her until she came by the force of her own will.

They lay like that for a long time and the only movement was Bet's tongue running over and over the fleshy little knob. After a while Kelly began to shiver a little and to sigh and suddenly, without either of them seeming to make it happen, a ripple began that changed into a wave. Bet felt it in her numbed tongue, one beat, very strong, and then another and another.

"Oh, oh, oh," cried Kelly, each time it beat. And then a wild sob burst out of her and she was crying.

Bet crawled up her body like a wall and put her face next to Kelly's. She pulled the covers up after her. They lay there in silence for a while and this time there was nothing jaunty about Kelly. She was exhausted.

After some time, as if to herself, Kelly said, "It's like being bled, isn't it? Like having the humors taken out of you."

A little later she said, "I don't let many women make love to me."

That irritated Bet. "But you obviously enjoy it."

"Not as much as making you come, lover."

"What's the difference?"

But Kelly changed the subject. "How did you and Norah make love?"

"What do you mean? The normal way. Like this." Bet was lying. Making love with Norah had never been like this.

"Normal?" Kelly laughed dryly, and then said, "Margo liked a dildo sometimes, a big one."

"That's too kinky for me."

Kelly laughed again, almost unpleasantly. "I forgot, you had the real thing once. Did Norah?"

"When I first met her, she still had him," Bet admitted. "His name was Daniel, they'd met in college. He was trying to be a writer, that kind of guy. Complicated. Brilliant. I couldn't stand him. I guess I might have been jealous of him . . . ."

But Kelly wasn't really interested. "I remember Jessica," she said. "She was tired of men. She liked it very slow and gentle; she liked to pretend she was asleep and have me seduce her. She could go on for hours after she got warmed up. One orgasm after another, I never saw anything like it."

"Norah and I . . . " Bet began, but suddenly it was too painful. She and Norah had been too inexperienced when they started, too unsure. And by the time they knew what they wanted, the first passion had crested and they were in a work and living relationship that took its toll in the everyday squabbling and the endless process of making up.

"Norah cheated on me, over and over," Bet burst out.

Kelly didn't say anything for a moment. Although she lay next to Bet her body felt remote, as if she had detached herself and were walking through another landscape. "That's a funny word, cheating—do you mean she had other lovers? Did you too?"

"Never . . . I thought about it once or twice, but it was really only Norah that I wanted. There was nobody like her."

Kelly stretched casually, and drew away slightly from Bet. "I always had lots of lovers when I was with Margo. She didn't care, as long as they weren't any of her friends. I'd go to the bars sometimes and take a woman home, give her pleasure and then come back to Margo."

"I'm not comfortable having more than one lover at a time," Bet said. It sounded stiff and resentful. "I mean, I wasn't with Norah . . . ." Norah was the only woman lover she'd ever had.

Kelly said nothing. She was drifting into sleep.

"Have you . . . slept with Mary Anne?"

"Umm-hmm."

"How was it?"

From the edge of sleep Kelly seemed about to answer, then she curled into Bet's side and put her arms around her, hugging her closely. "Good night, baby," she murmured. "Sleep tight."

• 8 •

KELLY WAS STILL ASLEEP WHEN BET WOKE UP IN THE MORNING.
The light in the bedroom was gray and grainy, like an inex-
pertly blown-up black and white photograph. Kelly's face
looked older in that light, the skin transparently thin and
chapped around the cheekbones and the chin. Kelly's
straight nose had become sharp—the rest of the face fell
away from its tip as if it were a pencil holding aloft some
crepey white material which grew looser and more crink-
ley at the edges, around the neck and corners of the eyes.

Bet stared at Kelly more fascinated than critical. As a
child she had sometimes come into her parents' bedroom
in the morning to wake them up. They had shadows and
lines all over their daytime faces and their mouths hung
open a little. Sometimes her mother's lips still had streaks
of pink or red; her father looked as if someone had
crayoned a light blueblack all over his chin and cheeks.
They gave off dark adult smells and when they woke up

their eyes seemed confused, not authoritative or exhausted or angry, but lost and almost sad, as if they had
just come from a special far-away and lonely place and
didn't recognize their daughter, even that they had a
daughter, at all.

She fell asleep again and dreamed that Norah had written a book. It came in the mail one day. *The Story of My
War* by Norah Goldman. At first Bet was angry. Mass Observation never asked *you* to keep a diary, she thought.
They were only interested in *my* notes. But when she
looked around her desk, all she found were a few scraps
of paper in her handwriting with the names of Norah's lovers on them. There were dates, exact dates, times and
places—something a detective might keep if she were
shadowing an errant wife. But no details. Bet found she
couldn't even remember the faces of the women Norah
had betrayed her with.

For a moment she was confused. Maybe they weren't so
important, she thought. Maybe I spent the entire war keeping notes on things that weren't important at all. Then she
was furious again, looking at the thick volume Norah had
sent her. It was at least five hundred pages.

Let's see what *you* have to say, she thought and opened
it. But to her surprise, it was all in Japanese.

When she woke up again Kelly was going down on her.
Sleepily and voluptuously Bet spread her legs and did nothing, marveling at the juicy ripeness of her cunt, like a can-
taloupe split open. It dripped and bubbled. Kelly's tongue
made a rough, enticing friction on the wet surface: sometimes it was a little needle of a tongue, tickling a tip only

millimeters in circumference; sometimes it was a fat hot animal of a tongue, embracing the swollen, the huge-feeling, the thumb-sized soft knot that was begging to be undone. Kelly's tongue came and went like armies advancing and retreating; and Bet was the citadel that couldn't help opening the doors and beckoning the army in, so that every retreat was less, every advance penetrated further in.

Kelly reached up and held Bet's breasts; the hard nipples brushed exquisitely against Kelly's chapped palms. The broken phrases began again, this time spilling hotly through her dry lips, pleading not to stop, not to ever stop. And all this time Bet's eyes were closed and after she had come her eyes were still closed, holding out, holding on to that memory of the very profoundest desire.

It was only when she felt Kelly move her head off her wet thighs that Bet reached for Kelly, but Kelly twisted agilely away and stood up by the side of the bed. She no longer looked sleep-weakened, elderly and parental, but like a lithe young boy. She had slight breasts and her rib cage stood out so you could see the bones. Her thighs and upper arms were strung with muscles, like a skinned rabbit.

"Come back," said Bet. "I want you."

"I need to take a shower, I feel sticky," said Kelly, and disappeared out the door. A few seconds later the water was running.

She didn't come back into the bedroom afterwards. Bet heard her in the kitchen, boiling water, then at the back door, letting Lulu in, talking to her.

"Hi," said Kelly when Bet came into the living room. She was brushing Lulu's coat. "I started to make some coffee and then realized I still didn't have any. Why don't we go out to breakfast?"

"Okay, sounds great." Bet was reassured at Kelly's friendly, matter-of-fact tone. She went to sit down beside her on the sofa and nuzzled at her neck. "That was so nice last night," she murmured. "I'm so happy you came."

She felt Kelly stiffen. "Yes, I like to sometimes," she said casually. "Come on, Lulu, you can come with us. Then we'll take you for a walk afterwards." Kelly rose and then sat down again, and took Bet in her arms. "Oh Bet, oh Bet, what am I going to do?"

"You mean about Mary Anne? She'll understand, I know she will."

"It's not that simple. I want both of you. Can I have both of you?"

"Does she know? About us?"

Kelly shook her head. "I used to joke to her about someone I was trying to get involved with—someone I said was the original hard-boiled egg."

"Oh thanks."

"Little did I suspect . . . " Kelly kissed Bet all over her face, tiny soft kisses. "I *do* like making love to you—the way you can just let yourself go like that."

Bet couldn't help herself. "How does Mary Anne make love?"

"Oh, I don't know . . . ." Kelly got up. "I thought of a great place we can eat."

Bet recognized the wracking sense of being measured and, perhaps, found wanting. Norah would never really tell her the details of her sexual encounters with other women, but after each betrayal Bet could tell that her expectations of sex had subtly altered. She wanted something different, something Bet didn't know how to give. Because she didn't know what it was.

Over breakfast Bet told Kelly a little about Norah and Eleanor. "Eleanor looks expensive—very short blond hair, blue eyes, cute little face, like a chipmunk's, with round cheeks, big teeth. She reminds me a little of Daniel, neurotic, artsy. She's a management consultant, but her thing in life is to collect."

"And so she collected Norah?"

"They met at some business women's lunch. Norah started going to things like that a few years ago. I can't stand them. I don't think Norah was interested at first, but then Eleanor started overwhelming her. Calling up with an extra ticket to the opera. Inviting Norah to a gallery opening. Nothing suspicious. She was polite to me on the phone. Her invitations were friendly—they just got more and more frequent. Would Norah like to meet so and so famous artist? Would Norah come with her to help her decide on such and such piece of Northwest Indian art. Norah had such a good eye; Norah's taste was marvelous; she wouldn't think of buying a painting at the opening unless Norah could give her opinion . . . ."

Bet was trying to make it sound amusing, but she noticed how strained her voice had gotten.

"Sometimes," Kelly said and stopped.

"What?"

"Sometimes it seems like you hate Norah. I don't understand it."

"I don't hate her. But she fucked me over, you can't deny that."

Kelly's gaze rested on Bet as if she'd never seen her before. "There's something I've been wondering," she said. "And that's how come you suddenly changed your mind about me after I told you I was moving in with Mary Anne."

It was the first time Kelly had spoken to her so coldly. Bet panicked. "What's so strange about it? I was coming to feel . . . a lot for you. The thought of losing you was so unexpected, it made me move more quickly. I'm not generally a fast mover, Kelly. Virgo, remember?"

Kelly kept staring at her. "I'm just afraid that if I give up Mary Anne, you'll lose interest and we'll be back where we started."

There was enough truth in this to make Bet lie instantly. "That's ridiculous. I'm sure I would have fallen in love with you anyway."

The words hung there.

"Are you in love, Bet?" Kelly asked cynically and sadly, and got up with the check. Bet didn't feel able to put a hand down to her wallet, much less to get up and stop Kelly.

Kelly went from the cashier to the pay phone and made a call with her face turned away from Bet. She didn't explain it when she came back. She looked restless.

"So, do you want to take a walk?"

"I guess." Bet felt helpless. She didn't know how the balance had shifted, but everything seemed in Kelly's favor now.

It was drizzling as they came out of the cafe. Neither of them said anything as they got into the car. Bet felt like a visitor from out of town dutifully being shown attention without real interest. Kelly drove to a large gray lake within the city limits. Once there Kelly seemed to recover some of her energy. She let Lulu out the back and immediately tossed her a stick. The dog ran right past it and kept running.

It was a dismal day. The forest around them looked thin and yet unkempt; second or third growth alder saplings scrabbled for light among the somber old firs that looked dusted with gray iron filings. The ground had more color than the trees. Wet russet leaves, big ones with a leathery, flexible look, were draped in great numbers over fallen logs, like lavishly unfurled bolts of cloth. Other leaves were a shiny olive color, oval shaped with a tough stem. Nothing crackled underfoot. It was too wet. The earth oozed damp, and so did the sky.

Kelly walked carefully ahead a little, directing her talk to the dog. "Nice out here, nice to be outside, isn't it, Lu? Come back and get the stick, good girl . . . ."

Bet walked behind her, brooding.

When they reached the lakeshore, a muddy bank clogged with sticks and leaves, Bet took Kelly's hand.

"I feel you're much more distant from me today," she tried.

"I don't want to be, but I am. I can't help mistrusting you a little, Bet."

"What do you mean?"

"I'm afraid of your jealousy."

Kelly's voice was low; her eyes searched the lake's flat gray surface as if looking for something she'd lost; her hand in Bet's was cool and slack.

At once Bet made a decision. She kept her voice calm and easy as she replied, "You don't have to be. No, I mean it. I've been through a lot with Norah, but I don't have to bring it to our relationship. I like Mary Anne, you know. As long as you and I can see each other . . . no, I won't be jealous. I don't want to be jealous anymore."

"You mean that, Bet?" Kelly turned to her with shining eyes; her whole face and posture had changed. "That's wonderful, that's great. Oh, you won't be sorry!"

Kelly let go Bet's hand and leapt a little, catching at a branch above their heads. The wind picked up slightly and broke the dull pewter of the lake into a more formal pattern of dark and light. Little droplets of water from the trees fell between them, on their faces.

"I'll tell Mary Anne right away," she said. "She'll understand."

Bet's heart shook like the wind and grew lighter, less troubled. She had never tried this with Norah, not in all their years together.

"You can come to the farm and I'll come to Seattle when I feel I need some culture!" Kelly was jubilant. "We'll go to art galleries. We'll get opera tickets and go to the ballet." Lulu jumped and nipped at her heels.

"Actually," said Bet. "I may not be in Seattle too much longer. I didn't mention it yesterday, but Norah and I are splitting up the business, I mean, I'm leaving it. I'm not sure what I'll be doing next." She felt Kelly pause and continued, with a pleasure that was partly cruelty, "I may visit my parents in California. Maybe I'll travel around there, get out of the Northwest for the winter."

"It's starting to rain harder," Kelly said, without emotion. She took a knit cap out of her pocket and pulled it over her ears. Her round pale face looked chapped and forlorn, almost ugly as she said, "You'd just go off like that?"

"I've never been to Europe either. Norah and I went to Hong Kong and Japan once for two weeks, a year or so ago, but we spent most of our time in warehouses and showrooms, and filling out forms and inspecting merchandise. We went to Mount Fuji, I think that's all we did for fun."

It was raining harder now. Lulu had retreated from the shore back to the damp and interesting woods. The lake was like a flattened piece of tin metal stretching before them and sheets of water cut sideways through the lowlying clouds.

Bet and Kelly stood apart, rain trickling down their faces; then they moved together, seeking each other's warm parts: cheeks, lips, fingertips.

"Please don't go, Bet," Kelly said. "I love you."

"If you knew me, you'd know I hate to go anywhere." She ran her fingers over Kelly's face, her closed eyelids, her hungry open mouth. "I love you too."

This time, she almost meant it.

But when they had returned to Kelly's car and roughly dried themselves, Kelly once again seemed restless and preoccupied. She looked at her watch several times, forcing Bet to look at hers too. It was just past noon.

"Want to go back to your house and light a fire?" Bet asked, taking Kelly's hand.

"Sure," Kelly said, squeezing back. Then she said. "I wish I could see my horses."

Bet flared up. "You called Mary Anne this morning. You said you'd come, didn't you?"

Kelly said nothing. She withdrew her hand to start the car and put it back on the steering wheel. Her profile was set and perfect and Bet was immediately remorseful.

"I'm sorry."

Kelly acknowledged her apology with a nod but didn't say anything.

"Look," said Bet. "If we're just going to make each other miserable, there's no reason to continue . . . ."

"We don't have to make each other miserable."

"But we will."

"I don't need to see my horses," said Kelly. "I'd rather spend the day with you."

"But listen, I've got to get back to Seattle anyway. I've got millions of things to do."

"I could go with you," Kelly said impulsively.

"No, no."

"We can have lunch before you go anyway. The ferry doesn't leave until almost four."

A strange exhilaration seized them. As if they had a stolen afternoon in which to do any number of things.

"There's a Dutch restaurant, or a Mexican . . . " Kelly said. "We could drive by them . . . ."

"Or, we could just go back to your house . . . ."

"After all," said Kelly, "we just had breakfast, didn't we?"

Outside Kelly's bedroom the winds tapped complicated messages with branches across the windows, percussionists in a fitful howling orchestra of wildness and need. Bet glimpsed snatches of sky through the window when they first came in the room: details of woodwork, a cobweb in the ceiling corner; a sock under the bed. Then it was as if the depth of her vision was reduced to the distance of an inch or less; all she saw was Kelly's skin; her eyes pored over it as if it were an illustration of a moonscape, pale, cratered, mysterious. The thinness of it was a strange delight, as if there were less that could separate them: it gave off a musky and intoxicating smell, part wet wood, part female.

They made love quickly, avidly, conscious of the lack of time, the need for hurry. The room was in a rainy twilight; the yellow covers gave off a glow that embraced them mouth on mouth, sweat on sweat, smell on smell. They were pasted together wrestling for control. Bet felt Kelly wanted to lay her out as an Ingres odalisque, to paint seductive sleepy lines with her tongue, but Bet wanted power more than the lazy pleasure of being the object of that tongue. She pushed Kelly flat against the mattress and lay over her, using her full height and weight; she spread Kelly's thin legs apart, making her want it, urging her on with the phrases that had gotten louder now in her mind: danger, need, want. She only came on Kelly's thigh as the last of Kelly's sighs died away, came rocking back and forth on Kelly's sticky skin, and she was slippery with sweat herself, in a trance.

Then it was over, time to go. Getting up to dress Bet felt woozy and out-of-body, her senses swimming at the end of her skin, like fish that won't be reeled in. She was sultry and heavy-headed; her mouth felt bare and stretched out of shape. She was half smiling.

Kelly lay there an instant longer. "Sometimes," she said, "I feel so much for you it's frightening. I almost like the sense of giving in to you when you get wild like that. It's overpowering."

"Maybe you're not so butch after all."

"I'm butch in a hundred ways you could never change. It's not just a sexual thing."

"Was your not letting me touch you at first shyness or policy?"

"I would have continued that way if you'd let me."

Bet laughed, not seeing Kelly's seriousness. "That's crazy. I know you like to come as much as I do—I feel it."

"It makes me tired," said Kelly. "Tired and vulnerable. It takes something out of me."

"I love that feeling though—voluptuous and erotic and wasted—don't you?"

"Not particularly." Kelly got up and began to put on her clothes. "I like feeling on top of things."

"Well, I don't believe in butch and femme," said Bet aggressively and cheerfully. "It's too limiting. I don't feel it applies to me at all."

Kelly said nothing. She moved around sluggishly and somewhat sullenly, looking for her boots, running her hands wearily through her hair.

"I don't think you really do either," Bet pressed her. "Do you?"

Kelly just looked at her, as if she didn't understand. Finally she said, "I'm butch and you're femme. And that's all there is to it."

They said good-bye in front of Kelly's house and made no plans to see each other. Bet was emotionally exhausted. It had only been twenty-four hours, but it felt like days she'd been with Kelly. It was almost a relief to part from her; she was sure Kelly felt the same.

"Well," said Kelly.

"It's been interesting," said Bet.

They hugged, almost impersonally, and then Kelly got on her motorcycle and Bet got into her car. They drove in opposite directions.

The rain clouds had dampened any sunset and made an early twilight. Outside Anacortes the oil refineries were lit up with hundreds of lights, magic and ethereal from a distance. As a child in California she had imagined that they were fairy palaces, that the illuminated smoke pouring from them came from genies on their way to perform wonders and spells.

But closer, the oil refineries looked more ominous, the night castles of polluting trolls. The red Texaco letters bled their reflection into the dark waters of Fidalgo Bay as Bet drove past.

◆9◆

WHEN BET CAME INTO THE SHOP MONDAY MORNING SHE FELT as if Norah could sense a change in her. As if Bet were giving off new sexual odors, as if some final intimacy between them were at last broken.

"What have you been up to?" Norah asked. She had on her wire rim granny glasses and her nose looked thin and pinched. Bet wondered if she had used to look as severe when Norah returned from one of her weekends away.

"What do you mean?"

"I tried to call you Saturday and Sunday."

"What for?"

"What do you mean, what for? Because. Because I thought we might get together and see a movie or something."

"I was away."

"Where?"

"Anacortes, if you really want to know." And Bet couldn't help smiling a little. Yesterday afternoon, after leaving Kelly, she'd felt something close to aversion. But already the power of memory was exerting its pull. By last night all she was remembering was the feel of Kelly's skin on hers.

Norah looked wounded, but didn't say anything more.

It was strange—there was some way in which Bet wanted to hurt Norah, wanted to show her own new invulnerability. She said, "I went to see Kelly. We fucked all weekend, it was great."

Norah got up deliberately from the desk and went into the shop. "Well, I hope you got what you were looking for—if that's all you want in a relationship."

Bet followed her and then stood with her legs apart, feeling bold and hard. "Yeah," she said, imitating someone—Clark Gable perhaps. "Maybe that's all I do want. It's amazing to make love with someone who really enjoys it." And she turned away.

"Eleanor and I don't just hold hands, you know," Norah countered. But it was a weak reply, to which Bet made no answer.

"You act like you just discovered sex," said Sylvia, when Bet dropped by her house late Tuesday evening. She was in the midst of an upholstery job, painstakingly removing the stained, threadbare velvet seats from six dining room chairs. Neat and fresh as ever she wore jeans, an oxford shirt and a sweater vest. She was chewing gum and listening to country western, loud, in the downstairs room where she worked.

"It's taken all my life, but I think I may be getting somewhere," Bet said. She had flung herself on a newly finished love seat and had stretched out, languorous as a cat.

Sylvia looked over at her ironically. "So you don't want a relationship anymore—you just want passionate sex?"

"I want both!" On her back, Bet threw out her arms, but then she dropped them, reconsidering. "Maybe I do just want sex with Kelly. I don't know. Sex makes me feel like we're having a relationship."

"But are you really suited . . . after what you said, about her being so butch . . . ?"

"Oh Sylvia, that doesn't matter anymore, not really. She lets me touch her now, she loves me."

"Well," said Sylvia, carefully pulling out upholstery tacks to Dolly Parton. "Then I'm impressed. But what about this other woman, the one on the island?"

"What about her? We can share Kelly . . . ."

"Share?" Sylvia lifted her eyebrows. "That doesn't sound like my Bet."

"This is different than with Norah. I feel like I have some control over the situation. Over how I feel."

"But you said Kelly is planning to move in with this woman. What's that going to be like for you?"

"I don't think she really will." Bet was surprised at how quickly and firmly she responded.

"But if she does . . . ?"

Bet sat up and picked up a tack that had bounced all over the floor. "Well, it wouldn't be the end of the world. After all, I don't want to live with her—and she says she wants to live with someone."

"Someone, it doesn't matter who?"

"Sylvia, we're not getting anywhere. You should be happy for me."

"I am, hon. I just don't want you to be hurt."

"But that's just it. I *was* hurt—I was hurting so bad I couldn't stand it. But now it's as if—I *feel* my body. I feel like I'm alive. I feel like I'm getting over Norah."

Sometimes when Sylvia looked at her Bet had the sense that Sylvia was really looking at some earlier version of herself; wanting to question, to help, to warn.

"You don't necessarily get over someone by getting involved with someone else. Unfortunately it's not that easy."

"Well I'm not going to get over anyone by sitting around and moping either." Bet tried to change the subject. "So, how's your love life?"

Sylvia gave a sputter that was like the sound an inflatable raft makes when someone jumps on it from a great height. "I told you, I've given all that up."

"But you're only forty-nine . . . ."

Sylvia pulled hard at the tacks. "My age has nothing to do with it."

"Why then? Aren't you ever going to have another lover?"

"No!" said Sylvia, yanking calmly. "And you know why? Because I'm fed up with dating and romance and flirting and all the rest of it. I'm fed up with love and I'm even fed up with sex." She turned to look at Bet, sprawled on the love seat. "The whole damn business is just too much fucking trouble."

Then she relented and gave Bet some carrot cake and listened to her go on about Kelly for two more hours.

♦ ♦ ♦

Norah had been thinking it over. She said to Bet the next day, "I believe you're making a mistake. You're getting involved with this woman for all the wrong reasons. On the rebound."

"Oh? You think I should wait a decent interval? Three years? Five years, ten years?"

"I think," said Norah tentatively, "that finding out about Mary Anne somehow upset you and so you flung yourself on the first woman who came along."

"Sometimes I can't believe we have these discussions . . . . If finding out about your girlfriends upset me that way, I would have started flinging myself, as you so gracefully put it, on people a long time ago. I don't go around analyzing your attraction to chipmunk cheeks, though I certainly could—so just lay off me."

"I don't think you know what you're getting into, Bet," Norah couldn't help continuing. She was wearing her earnest look, what, in more flippant times, they had called her Mrs. Freud face.

"Norah, you're driving me crazy! You do *not* always know what's best for me, even though you think you do."

Norah moved agitatedly around, trying to calm herself through the rearrangement of some Japanese baskets. "I've always depended on you to be the cautious one," she finally said in a small voice, and then went into the office and shut the door.

It was one of those horrible days when Bet couldn't stay angry and couldn't feel numb enough either, when the dart hit the target over and over again, each time with a needle-sharp stab: loss, loss, loss.

She didn't understand it. This fight was no worse than any they'd had lately, yet Bet was so upset she finally had to leave the store. She went outside and down to the canal, sat for a while on the bank tossing pebbles into the water. Had she become involved with Kelly so she could throw it in Norah's face, so she could punish her? And why was it so terrible for Norah that Bet was being sexual with someone? She should be happy.

The last time Bet and Norah had made love was over a year ago, during their brief visit to Japan. They had gone to see about importing some new lines for the shop, and because Norah wanted to. Norah was crazy about everything Asian, and especially Japanese. For a year before the trip she went to language classes, read books, saw travelogues, interrogated other visitors. When they got to Tokyo Norah was the one who immediately took charge. She made the appointments, marked up the guidebook, held on to the hotel key and the airline tickets.

Bet was in a state halfway between nightmare and utter disbelief. Once she had been in Tijuana, but this was nothing like that.

It was humid and soggy and there were millions of people. If she were to carry away one image of Tokyo it would be of the white-gloved fingers of men on the train platforms, pushing the last stray body parts into the trains before the doors closed.

Everything was so tiny.

Their hotel room was hardly bigger than their bathroom at home; the food came on miniscule plates in diminutive portions, delicate and insubstantial as doll food on doll dishes.

Norah was absolutely delighted with it all, or she would have been, if she hadn't had to drag Bet around. They went to department stores and small shops, visited show-rooms and warehouses. Bet didn't understand how a culture that seemed to delight in simplicity could at the same time produce so many things, so many souvenirs and gim-cracks, so many plastic models of food (spaghetti, choco-late sundaes, pork chops), so many electronic games and toys. When they walked down the Ginza her head spun.

At night it was even worse. Norah wanted to explore the discos and nightclubs, wander the streets bathed in neon, and poke her head in everywhere. If Bet went with her, it was only because she was too frightened to stay back at the hotel in the sweaty little room that reminded her of a coffin.

Only at the end did they get out of Tokyo. They spent a night at a lakeside resort on their way to Mount Fuji. They stayed in a traditional Japanese inn with tiled roof, wooden beams and rice paper walls. Their room was sim-ple: screens and a tatami mat, a low black lacquered table and, in an alcove, a scroll and flower arrangement. Their window looked out on a landscaped garden with pools of red and yellow carp, with waterfalls, with iron lanterns hanging from the eaves of the other buildings.

They took a bath almost as soon as they got there.

The water for the communal women's bath was sup-plied from hot springs; the room with the wooden tubs had a tile floor and plants in boxes and pots. Through the steam Bet saw perhaps half a dozen women talking with each other, from time to time looking curiously at Bet and Norah.

She didn't think she'd ever been so conscious of her own body, or of Norah's, as they changed out of their clothes and went into the bath room to soap themselves before entering the tub.

It wasn't that Norah looked especially beautiful or different. She was small and compact, but her torso was large in proportion to her legs, which were rather skinny and knock-kneed. Her smooth shoulders were a little rounded and her stomach was visibly convex. Her breasts were the size of large grapefruits, with dark brown nipples. Her frizzy hair was gathered into a ponytail and her skin was a warm olive color.

But Bet was also conscious of her own body. She was conscious because she saw Norah was conscious. There in that bath room full of naked women, Bet and Norah saw each other. Wanted each other.

The heat of the tub was tremendous, overpowering, and yet, for the first time since she'd arrived in Japan, Bet had a sense of being at peace, at home in her self. All around them the women talked quick Japanese, but Norah didn't try to talk with them. Her eyes were on Bet and Bet's were on her, sliding away, finding each other again.

Flushed and desiring, they went back to their tatami room in an erotic heat and fell upon each other, almost as if they were strangers, as if they'd never touched each other before. In that one late afternoon, before a discreet knock from a woman bringing dinner made them fall apart, they learned things they'd never known about each other. The intimacy was almost frightening; it was so unexpected and so violently *close*.

It must have been frightening. For they had never re-peated it, never done anything again that would bring them anywhere near it. After climbing Mount Fuji the next day they had to make their way back to Tokyo, back to the humid, frenzied streets, back to the subway trains and the men with the white gloves, scientifically packing human flesh into sterile containers, back to the hotel to pick up their bags, back to the airport to fly home to Seattle.

They quarreled furiously on the flight home about Bet's inability to be adventurous and Norah's insensitivity to anyone's feelings except her own. The conflict was more bitter for having to be suppressed on the plane; by the time they arrived at Sea-Tac they were no longer speaking. And immediately after that a profound change came into their relationship; they went their own ways more often than before. Norah kept up her Japanese lessons; she made new friends, went out more frequently at night. Bet stayed home and read and was lonely. She resisted this new life of Norah's and the resisting left her no energy to make a new life for herself.

But perhaps what they had both been resisting was the passion that had overwhelmed them at the Japanese inn, that had brought them, two long-time lovers, into the kind of intimate contact they once had longed for and now no longer did.

·10·

SNOW HAD FALLEN IN THE SKAGIT VALLEY SINCE BET HAD BEEN to Anacortes the weekend before. It lay in white patches by the side of the road and was spread across the fields like a thin coating of blue and pink confectioners' sugar on a chocolate cake. Over in the distance the winter sun was setting, a small coral fingertip loosing its last crooked hold on the horizon.

It was a cold whitish dark by the time Bet reached the turnoff at Mount Vernon, and Bet was cold too. She considered stopping for coffee, but the need to see Kelly was stronger. She didn't understand this urgency, but it was in her upper arms and in her thighs and in her breasts and abdomen, all the places she would press against Kelly when they met again.

She knew she was happy, but it was a happiness that was insecure and frightened, that needed continual reassurance. Kelly was going to move to the island, but she hadn't moved yet. There was still time to stop her, to make her understand. Kelly said she'd given notice at her job; Kelly said she was going to move right after New Year's. But that was still three weeks away.

Bet drove down Commercial Street and was warmed by the decorations tonight, not disgusted. They made a brightness, a determined cheerfulness against the dark night. She was afraid that Kelly wouldn't be there, even though they'd arranged this on the phone. Kelly had said she'd thought of going to the island this weekend. "You can go on Sunday," Bet had said, not pleading, trying to sound fair and unconcerned. "We'll have dinner Friday night and be together all day Saturday. You can go over Saturday night if you want."

She wasn't jealous, she wouldn't be jealous. The only way to keep Kelly was not to be jealous. This was an opportunity to change, to not be like she had been with Norah, to be larger and more generous.

"That's only one day with the horses," Kelly said reluctantly, but she agreed. "Yes, come up. I really want to see you, touch you."

That had made up for the reluctance. So much so that Bet had even been able to joke, "Some women just got to compete with other women. I got to compete with horses too."

Kelly had laughed at that.

Bet saw the lights on in Kelly's house and parked. She'd said, "Don't bother about dinner. I'll bring everything." And she had, everything from sourdough bread and pate to nicoise olives and radicchio and fennel for salad, to half a salmon and a spinach pasta. She'd left work early to shop at the market; everything had looked so wonderful, she had wanted to touch every vegetable, smell every breath of fish and fresh bread. The Spanish market had smelled of corn tortillas and chile; the Middle Eastern store had sent out gusts of coriander and curry. She'd bought coffee partly for the pleasure of going into the shop, and a linzer-torte from one of the bakeries. She'd bought a Blanc de Pinot Noir and a Riesling because, at the last minute, she'd thought, Maybe Kelly won't go Saturday night.

Bet went up to the house with her bags and backpack. Even the dog barking seemed welcoming, as was the so-prano of Joan Sutherland trilling from the living room. It had been so long since she'd been happy to see someone, to come home to someone.

"Bet!" and for a moment it was just as Bet had imagined. Kelly hugged her and swept her inside, took all her pack-ages and laughed at their quantity. "What's this, and what's *this*? Oh my god, you shouldn't have." Lulu jumped up and down, barking, and the two white cats ran back and forth through her legs, smelling the salmon.

"Oh my god," said Kelly again, kissing Bet's face, kissing her neck and cold hands. "And here I was just about to write you a note if you didn't get here soon."

"A note? About what?" Everything in Bet grew very still.

"Tam called an hour ago to say Glory was limping a little. If we leave right this instant, we can catch the five o'clock ferry."

"But the food . . . "

"We'll take it with us," said Kelly, already starting to turn off the lights in the house. "Mary Anne is always glad of some food."

"No!" shouted Bet, and then, when she saw Kelly's face, she continued more quietly. "You can't do anything about

Glory tonight. Kelly, be reasonable. Tomorrow is soon enough. You can take the early ferry, the dawn ferry if you want. Just don't go tonight. I mean, it doesn't make sense."

"Well," Kelly hesitated. "Maybe you're right. It's dark and everything . . . ."

"Tam's inexperienced too," Bet said firmly. "It might be nothing."

Kelly nodded. "Okay, I'll call her and tell her just to watch it overnight." She went back to turn on the lights and then to the telephone.

Bet took her bags into the kitchen and began unpacking, trying not to listen. Kelly was talking to Mary Anne, explaining that she'd be over in the morning. Nothing about Bet being at her house.

"Have you told Mary Anne, are you going to tell her about us?" Bet had asked Kelly on the phone earlier this week.

"I mentioned something about it."

"Doesn't she care?"

"She didn't seem to mind that much."

Of course not, Bet thought now. When Kelly is moving into her house in a few weeks. Why should she mind? She has no idea what's gone on between Kelly and me—the letters and the phone calls, the sexual intensity. Kelly hasn't told her anything about it.

In the kitchen Bet tried to recapture her good mood and excitement. She caught herself banging around the pots and decided to open the wine. It would be a nice evening; she'd make it nice.

After a few minutes Kelly came into the kitchen and took a glass of wine. "Mary Anne doesn't think it's that serious. She looked at Glory's hoof and it might just be a pebble or something. I need to teach Tam how to pick out and clean the hooves better. It's really important."

"So maybe you don't need to go over so early tomorrow."

"Ummm," said Kelly. "Delicious wine. Where'd you get it?"

"At the market."

"At the market? You went shopping at the market? You're wonderful!" Kelly came over and hugged her, then went pawing through the packages. "Seattle's market is so fantastic. And look at all this stuff. What's this fish, salmon? I love salmon. Oh Bet!"

Kelly's pale face grew red with pleasure; she kissed and nuzzled Bet's neck, then raced back into the living room to change the record, returned singing *Tosca* and offered to help cook, ended by just eating pate and bread.

They had dinner, and drank the two bottles of wine. Kelly drank most of the second one. They listened to *Tosca* and *La Boheme* (twice) and even *Aida*. They started making love on the living room floor and moved to the sofa, then to the bed.

And yet, from the beginning, their sexual responses were out of sync. Perhaps it was the wine, but there seemed to Bet something a little out of control about Kelly when they finally got into bed. Her hands were rough, she was pushy. She seemed impatient at Bet wrestling with her, trying to hold her own; she said, in a voice that had a new harshness in it, "Oh no you don't."

Bet panicked; she didn't want to spread her legs. They fought and Kelly climbed on top of her and held her down, put her hand between Bet's legs and her mouth on Bet's mouth. The mouth smelled of wine, the fingers were too demanding; they squeezed at her almost painfully, for she wasn't wet enough.

She couldn't seem to get wet, but Kelly didn't act as if that mattered. She ground down on Bet, in a rhythm that was made jerky by Bet's attempts to free herself, to shift around.

"Stop, Kelly, this isn't working, it's hurting," Bet said.

But Kelly kept on, oblivious, for several more minutes until she finally said, "What's the matter?"

"I thought you'd never ask." Bet shoved Kelly off and moved away.

"Don't be mad, Bet. What's wrong?" Kelly leaned over her, tender, solicitous.

In spite of herself, Bet started crying. Why was she so upset? She didn't know.

Kelly cuddled her. "Hey, don't worry, it's okay, lover. We all have our off days . . . ."

Something in Bet wanted to protest, but this wasn't an off day until you made it off. But she kept quiet and let herself be held. She couldn't bear to face the fact that something between her and Kelly was wrong, and that it might always be wrong.

Bet dreamed she was in the office at the store, doing the accounts. It was late at night and at first there was a comfortable feel to the dream. She was in a familiar place, everything was as it should be. The lamplight shone in an oval on the faint green piece of paper as she went up one column and down another, doing it all in her head, simple arithmetic.

But after some time she began to doubt herself—the numbers weren't adding up as they should, the totals conflicted, something was gravely wrong. Was the mistake Norah's—or Bet's? She realized that she needed the calculator for this, she couldn't do it herself, she wasn't smart enough. But just as she was reaching for the calculator, she heard a noise and froze.

Someone was coming in the front door.

Bet turned off the light and got under the desk, she shrank into the smallest bundle she could make of herself.

There were footsteps—and two women's voices. The conversation was desultory, the kind people have just before they go to bed. They weren't at all suspicous that anyone might be in the shop.

"Bet and I have an arrangement," Norah said. "She understands that I need other lovers. I'm that kind of person, it doesn't have anything to do with her."

"But you'd never leave her, would you?" The voice sounded like Eleanor's, but Bet wasn't sure.

"Oh, I don't know, someday maybe. I've certainly thought about it." Norah sighed. "It's all so complicated. I mean, I really am *fond* of Bet. And we're business partners too." It sounded like Norah was taking off her clothes. She was perfectly relaxed, listing for her lover all the pros and cons of the relationship with Bet. "She's stable, she's kind; she's intelligent and actually fairly perceptive. But—well, she doesn't take risks; she's not at all ambitious; I don't know, she *lacks* something, she always has."

"And she can't make you feel like this, can she?" There was a sound of nuzzling, wetness, lust.

"Oh," said Norah. "I love it when you do that."

Bet realized they were about to make love. She wanted to cry out, to turn out the lights but at the same time she didn't want to see them or let them know that she was there.

Their voices got lower and lower—there was only a kind of grunting. Like animals.

Bet felt as if she were hiding in a bomb shelter. She wanted to get out and stretch her stiff limbs but she was afraid of being killed. She hid because that was the only way to protect herself from the whine of the rockets and the splintering sound of the glass, the thunder of concrete and stucco crumbling around her.

She waited and waited but the attack never came. Finally she got up and crawled outside. The light was so bare on the world, with no houses to break it into streets and neighborhoods. Everything stood out in sharp relief, from the light snow dusting the rubble to the white clouds against the agate blue sky. It's over, thought Bet, the war is over, just as the sirens began to wail again.

Bet stopped herself from dreaming any more of the same dream, but later while she was asleep she heard Mary Anne say, as clearly as if she were in the same room, "What *are* we going to tell her?" The warmth and weight of her voice pressed down like an iron over the words, smoothing them back and forth. "Poor Bet, poor Bet. She never gets what she wants."

Kelly answered immediately. "We'll have to hide it from her. We'll have to lie, at least at first, at least for a little while. She wouldn't understand. We have to protect her."

"I can't lie," said Mary Anne, and now she sounded weary and resigned. "No, someone is going to have to tell her the truth."

"I'm warning you—she's not ready to hear it."

"What truth?" Bet screamed. "What happened?"

But she knew it already . . . .

Norah had died in the bombing. Norah was gone forever.

Kelly didn't wake up for the dawn ferry and Bet, who was making coffee, hoped that she might have given up the idea of going at all. They could have the whole day to themselves then, try to straighten some things out. Almost optimistically she wandered around Kelly's house looking at things, wondering what Jessica had been like, how she had filled the space. Was the idea of living with Kelly really so impossible?

After a while she heard Kelly in the bathroom, running the shower and making a lot of noise. Finally Kelly emerged, fully dressed in Levis and a flannel shirt, her hair wet and plastered to her head, but beginning to spring up in curls. She looked big-eared and vulnerable as she took the cup of coffee Bet offered.

"I was thinking," said Kelly. "Why don't you come with me to the island this morning?"

"I don't know about that. What about Mary Anne? It doesn't seem fair to her."

"But you're part of my life too," Kelly said, as if she'd been rehearsing this argument with herself in the shower. "If I'm going to live there it's got to be my place too. I should be allowed to have my own friends."

"You know, Kelly," Bet said in a low voice, "at some point you'll have to make a choice."

"This is all so crazy." Kelly sprang away and started pacing up and down the room with her deliberate swagger. "A month or two ago I had no one. I was desperately, horribly lonely. I'd tried suggesting an affair to Mary Anne and that hadn't worked. Then I met you and went head over heels. When you didn't respond, when you seemed scared of me . . . "

"I was scared of you . . . it was so immediate and strong."

"I thought you hated me. If you had only come up here that Thanksgiving."

"I'm here now though. It's not too late."

"I've made a commitment to Mary Anne and Tam."

"But you have to follow your true feelings."

"And the farm, and the horses . . . " Kelly looked at Bet almost mockingly. "You don't have anything to offer me, Bet."

Rage flushed through her but she ignored it. "You can have as many futons as you want."

Kelly laughed and put her arms around Bet. "Come to the island. We'll just stay the day. It's so beautiful there. I know Mary Anne would like to see you. She likes you. You could take a walk or something while I look at Glory . . . then we'll come home tonight, we'll make love however you want to."

Against everything that told her this was idiotic, bound to cause needless grief and trouble, certain to end in disaster, Bet closed her mind. She said that yes, she would go.

·11·

THEY TOOK THE ELEVEN-FIFTEEN FERRY. THE SUN SHONE HARD,
beads of heat encased in cool salt water rained down on
their faces. The sky was a strong ceramic blue; the water
darker blue with light scattered through the crest of every
wave. Out on deck the wind was just short of freezing at
the bow. The fir-covered islands gave way around them,
while iridescent black cormorants followed the leader
from rock to rock.

It was an alive feeling to be outside, looking down at
the way the ferry cut through the water, sending up white
fireworks of spray before it. Kelly and Bet stood close together and whispered in each other's cold ears. They
kissed and didn't care who saw them.

It took an hour crossing. As they neared the island they
went back down to the lower deck to find Kelly's
motorcycle. They kissed again and rubbed against each
other; a furtive sense of betrayal charged all their
movements. Soon they wouldn't touch at all.

Off the ferry, Kelly roared up the hill and straight down the road that led through the center of the island to Mary Anne's turnoff. Everything about the island had a different feel in this sunlight. The greens were thick and emerald-blue. The fields glistened with moisture from the melting snow. All of it was lush and fertile and radiant.

It was only when Mary Anne came out of the house that Bet realized she hadn't known Bet was coming.

Bet was embarrassed, then furious at Kelly. She'd done this on purpose, just to test them! But no, Kelly seemed embarrassed too; glancing from one to the other she made a soft, coughing sound and said, "Bet came with me for the day."

"It's good to see you, Bet," said Mary Anne warmly. "How are things with Norah, with the store?" She looked bigger and more maternal than Bet remembered; her brown eyes in her deeply freckled face seemed absolutely kind.

Bet nodded. "Okay, fine." She felt a lump rising in her throat. If only there were someone she could talk with about Norah. If only Kelly weren't here and she could really talk to Mary Anne.

"I'm just baking some bread," Mary Anne said. "I'd offer you some coffee, but I just realized a few minutes ago that I'm out. I was thinking of going to get some at the store. I don't get it at the deli anymore."

"Because of Judy," Kelly put in, then looked guilty. She suddenly saw Tam in the pasture and went calling after her.

"Judy's taking it hard," said Mary Anne. She pushed her hair back from her face and smiled at Bet ruefully. "She was bound to, wasn't she?"

Bet found herself nodding. "That's too bad." She felt as if she were in a play. From the corner of her eye she saw Tam racing towards Kelly with a delighted face, calling, "Her foot's okay today." Suddenly the pain of it, of hurting Mary Anne, of being hurt, of losing Kelly, of losing Norah came over her and she had to get away.

"Maybe I could go to the deli and get some coffee. Anything else?"

"Oh, would you, Bet? That'd be great, their coffee's so much better. You can take the truck if you want."

"I'm in no hurry," said Bet. "I'll walk."

The deli was aromatic with spice and espresso, dim after the bright winter sun. Judy couldn't conceal her surprise at seeing Bet. "What are you doing here?"

"Visiting Mary Anne with Kelly . . . I wanted to get some coffee, half a pound of Guatemala, ground."

Judy came around the counter, tall, a little awkward. She was wearing a white apron over her neat crewneck sweater and jeans. Her fresh eager face looked closed and sad. "Kelly. Oh. You came with Kelly."

Judy called back to someone in the kitchen, "Moon, I'll be back in a minute," and motioned Bet out the deli door. "You don't mind talking about it, do you? I haven't had anyone to talk about it with. And—it's been pretty painful."

She had been leading Bet in the direction of a grassy bit of land with some trees. Now she pulled off her white apron and made Bet sit down with her on it. "You're the only person I can talk to because you don't live here. Everybody else, they'd just gossip."

She looked at Bet, suddenly shy. "You do want to hear about it, don't you?"

There was nothing Bet wanted less, but she nodded.

"It was back over Thanksgiving and Mary Anne was having this big potluck, and she was going to have fifteen or twenty people over, all with their kids and everything. You know the kind of thing, with everybody running around and stuffing themselves and then just sitting and burping all afternoon. It wasn't that I didn't want to go, but I was in this very tricky place with my book, at a very crucial part—I had made this incredible connection between tenure track and railroad track and that had led me to the history of the Chinese in America and . . . "

Judy turned her dark blue eyes on Bet; the thick lenses magnified her pain. "I just couldn't force myself to go to Mary Anne's. I needed silence and I was fasting too. I just wanted to be alone. But then, by about Saturday night I was exhausted and had just finished my chapter and wanted to tell somebody about it. I'd told Mary Anne I'd be over when I was done, so it wasn't like she wasn't expecting me at any moment."

Judy paused and took off her glasses and wiped her eyes. Her finely cut lips tightened. "It was late Saturday night, dark, and I was riding my bike so it didn't make any noise when it came up the driveway. They were on the porch—I knew it was Mary Anne because of her hair, even though she was lying down. And I knew it was Kelly too—just because of the way she *is*—I just saw this kind of silhouette, Mary Anne lying down with her legs up and spread and Kelly's face down there." Judy began to cry. "I mean, it was so awful to look at them making love—that never even happened when Jocelyn got involved with that sociologist. Jocelyn just told me about it—I never *saw* them doing it."

Bet saw it now too, saw it and felt it as a pinching of her own genitals, as if someone had poured cold water on her vulva and stuck clothespins on her labia.

"It wasn't like I thought Mary Anne and I would be together forever," said Judy, leaning into Bet's shoulder and making it wet. "I knew I would have to move back to the mainland eventually—I know there's not enough stimulation here. I can't keep working in the deli and I hate animals, especially dairy animals, but I really loved Mary Anne. I never thought that she'd betray me. I thought I'd finally found someone I could trust, really trust."

Bet didn't cry, but she easily could have. Only anger stopped her, a white-hot disgusted anger that evaporated the tears as they formed. She hadn't been able to trust Norah in the end, that was the worst part, not being betrayed—but not being able to trust her. Maybe there was no trust in the world. Only betrayal, lying and disguising and the pure, awful deceitfulness of people saying one thing and doing another.

She held Judy and rocked her, feeling the woman's strong, slender limbs, angry for her sake too. She fished for a handkerchief in her pocket and handed it to Judy, who coughed and sighed and gradually recovered herself.

"I'm sorry," Judy finally said. "I've been doing this a lot lately." She looked up at Bet's face, from where she lay nestled against her jacket, and asked, "How do you feel? I can't believe you're here visiting Mary Anne with Kelly."

"I can't believe it either," said Bet and laughed shortly.

"I never knew you were involved with Kelly until Mary

Anne told me. I'd gone home that Saturday night, you know, completely beside myself. I was afraid to go over there on Sunday because I thought I'd meet Kelly and then all of a sudden Mary Anne turns up at my house saying she needs to talk to me. She was honest at least. She said she'd liked Kelly for a long time and suddenly it had become sexual."

"Did she say . . . she was in love with Kelly?"

"No . . . she just said they got along. That Kelly was going to move to the island. Can you believe it? One night and they've got it all settled."

"But Mary Anne knew about me? She knew that Kelly and I had been . . . seeing each other?"

"The way she described it, it was no big deal to either you or Kelly, especially to you. She said that Kelly'd had a little crush on you, but that you weren't interested. Was it more than that?"

Bet found it difficult to answer. "No, not much more," she said finally.

"You're lucky then," said Judy. "Mary Anne and I had been together over four months. I really cared about her. I thought we had some commitment. She says we'll still be friends, but I don't see how. Not with Kelly always around."

They got up and brushed themselves off.

"I guess I'd better get the coffee," Bet said. The feeling of numbness was upon her again, preventing her from showing either anger or grief.

"Thanks for listening," said Judy, touching her arm gently. "You're just staying the day today? You want to come over to my place later? I could make you dinner. It's really nice there, in the middle of the woods."

Bet shook her head. "I've got to get back to Seattle tonight."

They walked back to the deli and Bet bought the coffee.

The cows were bunched around their almost empty wooden feed trough in the small enclosure near the barn. Their brown and white coats were rough and they looked skinny and sad. Some of them were staring vaguely at the ground, as if recalling the fresh green grass of spring and summer. Others, more stoic, simply chewed. All of them stared at Bet as she came up the drive and the younger ones took shy ballet steps quickly away.

"Fiona, Lydia . . . ," Bet tried. They had dark rings around their eyes that, together with their leaf-shaped ears, made them look continually surprised and watchful. Animals didn't care so much what you said; they mainly observed your movements.

She went into the barn, to be alone, to postpone the moment when she would have to see either Mary Anne or Kelly. It was damp inside, smelling of manure and hay. The small-paned windows had the translucent look glass has against dark wood when the light coming in is pale and cold, like trays of ice set upright in the wall.

The small shed attached to the barn was where Mary Anne stored the milk and made cheese and yogurt. Bet heard its door creak and instinctively backed into the darkness a moment. Then she left the barn.

Over in the pasture Kelly and Tam were working with Glory. They both wore jeans and flannel shirts under down vests. Except for Tam's glossy curls it wasn't easy to tell them apart. Bet moved up to the fence where she could see and hear them better.

They had the young chestnut horse on a long line attached to the halter and stood driving her in circles. Kelly held a long willow switch.

"Walk, Glory," said Kelly and flicked the switch lightly on the horse's hindquarters. "Trot, Glory," she said and flicked the switch again, giving the horse the merest tap.

"Whoa, whoa." To Tam she explained, "When Glory understands what the switch means you won't have to use it. This is to get her used to your voice commands, before you start riding her. Two year olds shouldn't be ridden too much anyway. Their bones are still developing. But this will make it easier when you start."

She gave the switch and long line to Tam. "You want to stand behind her a little, Tam, so you can keep her going and keep her from turning to face you. She'll want to face you or want to come to you until she understands she's supposed to travel in a circle around you."

Tam nodded eagerly and applied the switch lightly to Glory's hindquarters at the same time she raised the lead line in her left hand. "Walk, Glory, walk, girl, go on." Glory turned and looked at Tam, her long intelligent face puzzled at the new voice giving directions. Tam switched her lightly again. "Walk, Glory, walk, walk."

Glory took a few steps forward. "Look, Kelly, she's walking!"

Kelly laughed. "Hit her again and tell her to trot."

Glory trotted, then walked again; finally she whoa'd up.

They went on like this for some time. Neither was aware of Bet standing at the fence.

Bet went inside the house and took a book from a shelf in the living room. It was a lesbian novel with two misty, purple-tinted forms in an embrace on the cover.

Mary touched Melissa's cheek gently, slid her hand gently yet tremulously over her shoulder and down until she almost touched Melissa's breast. Melissa sighed, quivering. "Mary, oh Mary, I've waited so long for this moment."

They locked gazes, emotion escalating as they realized they no longer had to hold back the deep feelings that they had both so long felt. "You're so beautiful, Melissa." Mary took Melissa's face again in her hands, stroking it with tender, delicate motions. They kissed for what seemed like forever, unutterably ecstatic at the discovery of this new-found bliss.

Bet put the book back and found one instead called *Your Horse and You.*

The horse evolved as a herd animal. He is instinctively familiar with a structured social order . . . . You must establish yourself as higher in the pecking order than the horse—you must make the horse think that certain things are your idea . . .

Your job as owner-trainer-handler is to substitute your will for the horse's will and to keep him under sufficient submission for control.

You want all his brilliance and nerve and spirit intact, and you want it to be yours for the asking.

Never lie to a horse. He won't forget it.

Bet wished she'd brought with her the book she'd been reading at home. It was a woman's diary of the nine hundred day siege of Leningrad during the war. Over a million people had died then, of starvation and disease.

But Vera Inber had lived to tell about it.

Suddenly very restless and made bold by the fact that no one was in the house with her, Bet left the living room and went upstairs. She went into the room she'd stayed in before and looked at it, then into the room where Kelly had stayed the last time. Both were clean and neat, almost exactly the same, except that Kelly's bed had a white chenille spread and Bet's had a quilt. Each bed was twin-sized and virginal, with a small reading lamp next to it.

Then Bet went into Mary Anne's room. It too had something of a chaste, feminine look. The room was painted white and had only a big maple dresser and a rocking chair next to the double bed with the brass bedstead. On the dresser were some photographs in frames. There were several of Tam at different ages, clowning and serious. Bet picked up the baby picture and looked at it carefully. There was also a photograph of a man that Bet thought must be Jack. He was heavily bearded and was wearing a wool knit cap down over his forehead; his eyes were blue and kind. There were no photos of Kelly or Judy or other women.

If I told her how I felt about Kelly, thought Bet vaguely. But no, she had never loved Kelly, not really. It was Norah she loved, Norah whose photograph was still in her desk drawer, a guilty secret. It was a young Norah, snapped one summer's day outside the cottage at Sylvia's. Norah with her small face almost hidden by her frizzy hair, a wicker basket of yellow roses at her feet and more roses climbing the trellis behind her.

Sylvia had taken the photo on a day when Bet hadn't been around. She'd given it to Bet after Norah and Bet had moved out. Norah probably didn't even know that Bet had it, that she took it out from time to time, trying to remember that happiness.

She went into Tam's room and lay down on the bed.

The last time Bet had been here Tam had taken her on a little tour of her treasures. There were two shelves above the small desk. One held a row of books, mainly overdue library books on horses. The other shelf was packed with small horse figurines and cut-out horses pasted to cardboard and propped up. On the walls were more color photographs of horses. Tam seemed especially fond of the straight-on views of the horses' faces. There were at least five of them and they all seemed to be looking right at Bet with intelligent but indifferent eyes.

The afternoon sun came in through the horse-patterned curtains and fell across the horse-patterned bedspread. Bet got under it and curled up like a ball. If she could just not think for a little while, just go completely numb, maybe fall asleep.

She didn't feel as if she'd slept but she supposed she had when she opened her eyes and found Tam looking at her.

"Are you sick?"

"No," said Bet, sitting up. "I was just tired. Is it late?" It seemed darker in the room and Bet had a panicky feeling, as if she had to get away, though she'd forgotten why.

"It's three or something," said Tam. "We're finished with Glory and I'm going to curry Nutmeg, but I just had to get another sweater." She sat down an instant next to

Bet on the bed. "My mom wants me to do the milking but I don't want to. I hate cows!" she burst out. "They're so stupid!"

She looked bigger than the last time Bet had seen her, broad in the shoulders like her mother but with larger hands and feet. Her wide freckled face burned with exertion and she gave off a smell of young, barely pubescent sweat. Kelly's in love with both of them, Bet thought, and then clamped that thought down.

"You like horses though."

"Horses are smart, you can ride them and make them do things, it feels like you're part of them. Cows just stand there and need to be milked all the time. They're ugly too, the way they're always chewing and chewing. Horses are in races."

Tam got up abruptly and took a sweater from the drawer. "Are you and Kelly going to stay here tonight?"

"No," said Bet, more vehemently than necessary.

"Kelly is."

"Kelly can do what she wants."

"Kelly is sleeping with my mom. She's going to move here after Christmas and we might buy another horse. Or she might let Nutmeg have another foal. You're just friends, aren't you? You and Kelly?"

"Yeah," said Bet. "But you'd better hurry before it gets dark outside."

"See ya," said Tam and raced out.

Bet got up and went to the bathroom, washed her face.

"Oh, there you are," said Mary Anne, coming up the stairs. She was wearing a soft sweater in sienna and gold that picked up highlights in her skin and hair. Beneath her commanding torso her legs were long and slender. She had a house, she had a daughter, she had a herd of dairy cows. "Did you take a nap up here?"

Bet nodded.

"Come on down and have some fresh banana nut bread. Did you get the coffee all right?"

"I think I left it in the living room. Sorry."

It wasn't Mary Anne she hated. Still, she had to get out of here before she did something unforgivable.

"Actually, I can't stay, Mary Anne. I've got to get back to Seattle tonight. I've, uh, got a date. Isn't there a ferry soon?"

"You'd have to leave right away." But Mary Anne's face cleared at the mention of the word *date*. Underneath her warmth she had been worried.

They went downstairs together and out to the porch. Mary Anne helped her with her coat and scarf.

"You'll have to come and visit us sometime soon," she said, a little uncertainly. It was obvious she suspected that more had gone on between Kelly and Bet than Kelly had told her, but she wasn't sure how much.

Bet wasn't going to tell her.

"Be sure and give my love to Norah," Mary Anne said, following her a couple of steps down the porch and then waving. "Bring her up sometime with you."

Bet went inside the barn. It was lit by a single bulb that cast shadows everywhere. It was very cold. Kelly and Tam were in the stall with Nutmeg.

"Neck, breast, withers, shoulders, forelegs, back, sides, belly, croup, hind legs—remember, that's the order. Curry her gently. We'll brush her vigorously afterwards, and then use the hoof pick like I showed you . . . . Oh hi, Bet. Where've you been all afternoon?"

"I'm going to catch the ferry. Can you give me a ride right now or should I hitchhike?"

Kelly just stared at her without saying anything.

Bet was surprised at the firmness in her voice. "I'll hitch then. No problem. See you around."

"Bet, wait. Of course I'll give you a ride. But, why leave right now?"

Bet was already walking out of the barn. "Because I only planned to spend the day. *We* only planned to spend the day. And the next ferry's not till late. And it appears you're staying overnight anyway."

Kelly followed her, trying to explain. "It's so hard to be over here and *not* stay, Bet."

"That's fine, just fine. But you shouldn't have dragged me over here then, saying we were just going to spend the day. Did you think I'd stay over too? And where was I going to sleep? Or have you figured out a way to sleep with both of us at the same time?"

She stomped over to the motorcycle and Kelly came after her. She pushed Kelly's arms away. "Just take me to the ferry, okay?"

Kelly got on and started the motor, then she leaned back and said, "We're so different, Bet."

Bet climbed on behind her. "We're different all right. You're a liar and I'm not."

"I've never lied to you."

"You've lied the whole time."

"You see things so differently."

"Just take me to the ferry, okay?"

Kelly roared forward and Bet had to lunge to hang on. She felt Kelly's body in front of her with desire and pain. How was it possible to love and not be loved back, to lose people over and over again?

They said nothing more until they reached the ferry landing. They were almost too late. The foot passengers had already boarded and the few cars were driving on. Bet would have to run for it.

"I'll call you," said Kelly as Bet hopped off the bike.

"Please don't."

"I love you."

"That's a funny way to end things."

"I do though."

"Go fuck yourself . . . ." And then she turned and saw Kelly one last time, lounging back on her bike, hair wind-blown above her straight profile . . . "lover," she whispered.

She ran and caught the ferry just before they untied the ropes and raised the dock.

$\cdot 12 \cdot$

SUNDAY IT SNOWED IN SEATTLE AND BET STAYED INSIDE AND read Vera Inber's *Leningrad Diary*.

16th September, 1941
It gave me a strange feeling when the phone rang and a fresh young voice said: "The telephone is disconnected until the end of the war." I tried to raise a protest, but knew in my heart it was useless. In a few minutes the phone clicked and went dead . . . until the end of the war.

Monday Bet didn't go into work in the morning. At about twelve her doorbell rang. It was Norah.

"Are you sick? Why didn't you call? I got worried, thought you might have been in an accident . . . you didn't answer your phone . . . ."

Norah advanced hesitantly into the room. She hadn't been to visit Bet once since she'd moved out and now, seeing Norah look around the room, Bet was aware how little she'd done to fill in the gaps. The futon sofa, the armchair and the end table with its lamp were the only furniture and all that was on the walls was an old poster that had once been Norah's.

"I can't believe you haven't done a thing to this apartment. You've got to snap out of this, Bet!"

Bet, who wanted desperately to admit to Norah that she was falling apart, that this was serious, froze up and said nothing.

"Oh, that's right, go ahead, stand there accusing me like you've always done. I put most of the energy into the apartment and now I've taken it away. It's all *my* fault."

It should have hurt, coming from Norah like this in the midst of her more recent pain, to know that Norah was right, that Bet was a complete failure at relationships, that no one would ever want her, ever, but it didn't. Bet was too numb for that.

Norah was beside herself. "Fine!" she almost shouted. "So don't tell me what's going on, what's wrong with you. Sit here and leave me alone at the store today and forever, answering the phone by myself and having to deal with all the customers. But I don't think it's fair—not at this time of year and you said you'd stick with it until the end of December."

Norah burst out crying and still Bet stood there, hands at her sides. It hurt her to see Norah in tears, but there was nothing she could do about it. She was like a corpse, frozen with grief.

Norah slammed out the door. And Bet went back to reading, this time from Harrison Salisbury.

The snow was piling up in the streets of Leningrad. It was growing colder and colder, the coldest winter anyone could remember. And yet paradoxically the cold helped the starving people of Leningrad, for it caused Lake Ladoga, thirty-five miles away, the largest lake in Europe, to freeze quickly and freeze deep.

They made a highway over the lake and they called it the Road of Life. Over the road came trucks and trucks full of supplies. It was never enough, it could never be enough. Not for two and a half million people. It was something. It was a lifeline, built across the ice.

In the evening Norah came back. "Hi," she said with forced cheerfulness. "I thought you might like to take a walk, get a beer or something."

"Okay." Bet pulled on an old pair of boots and threw on another sweater before she put on her jacket. She tugged her cap down low over her forehead without glancing in the mirror. She knew she must look horrible, makeshift, ill.

Norah wore a bright purple ski jacket over black wool pants tucked into high leather boots and looked beautiful. Her thick gloves and scarf were handknit from nubby purple and black wool, and on her frizzy hair perched a black beret with a purple pin in the shape of a comet.

The snow had continued to fall all day. A few flakes still drifted down but it had stopped for the most part, leaving another two inches on Sunday's three. Few cars were on the road; evidence of earlier driving was left in the form of woozy S curves on the downslopes of the hills.

Norah said she'd walked up from the store. "There wasn't much business today because of the weather. I didn't mean to make such a big deal about your not being there."

Bet nodded. They were at the top of the hill; looking down they saw the blue-gray Ship Canal and across Lake Union the lights of the city. Everything was lovely in the snowy twilight; not like Leningrad where frozen corpses went by on sleighs, sometimes only wrapped in paper and string.

"How about the Buckaroo?" Norah asked.

Bet nodded again. She still hadn't found anything to say. Now a sharp pain went through her. Kelly would have liked this tavern, with its neon cowboy on a bucking bronco against the violet sky.

"I didn't mean to attack you this morning," Norah began, when they'd taken their beers over to an empty wooden booth. She hesitated and took off her beret, shaking out her hair. She was really and truly beautiful, Bet thought objectively. She remembered Kelly's aquiline profile and then her front tooth and thought of something that had plagued her: in those early photos with Margo and the horse in Vermont, Kelly's tooth hadn't been crooked. Had she fallen somewhere along the line, or had someone punched her in the mouth?

"It's just that I've been worried about you," Norah went on earnestly. "And seeing the apartment, how it's so bare and everything—I'm just worried about what's happening to you, what's going to happen to you."

"Nothing's happening to me," said Bet dully. "I'm fine."

Norah looked even more earnest. "But what are you going to do in January? Here it is mid-December and you haven't said. Are you looking for another job or what?"

"I might go somewhere." It sounded unconvincing even as she said it. She tried, with more enthusiasm, "I might go to California and visit my parents or something."

"Ten minutes with them and that would be enough. That's not a solution, Bet, it's not a plan."

"Why do I have to have a plan? Why can't I just . . . travel around? Or why can't I just vegetate if that's what I feel like. What do you care?"

"If that's all you're going to do you might as well keep working for a while. Until you decide what to do."

"No."

"But Bet, think about it. It's going to be hell for me—the year end sales, trying to hire someone, inventory, everything. And you've said yourself you don't know what you're doing." Norah's tone had become almost wheedling and she placed a slender ringed hand on Bet's. "Won't you stay a little longer? Please?"

It was hard to resist her. Bet focused her eyes on a knotty pine wall, on the knots. "I told you. December 31st. That's it."

Norah jerked her hand away. "I don't know what you think you're going to do anyway," she muttered. "You don't really care about anything. You're the most boring person I know."

Bet didn't answer. Of all the things Norah had ever said to her, somehow this was the worst. For it was true. Norah had filled her life; without Norah there was nothing left.

It was pathetic.

"Bet, I'm sorry. I didn't mean that, really. I'm just . . . *worried* about you."

If only she could give Norah what she wanted; if only she could, right now, reach across the table, take Norah's hands and crush them in her own, tell her, "Yes, I'll keep working with you until I find something else to do with my life. Yes, even your friendship is the most important thing in the world to me."

Instead she sipped painfully at her beer.

"I've been thinking," said Norah, after a few minutes had passed. "That maybe we should see a mediator . . . no, not a therapist, I know how you feel about therapists— though I've been seeing someone and it wouldn't hurt you either."

"You're probably only seeing someone because Eleanor sees someone."

"It wasn't Eleanor's idea that I see a therapist. It was my idea," said Norah, flushing slightly. "I have some things to work out, about . . . monogamy . . . ."

"Hah," said Bet. "I could have told you that."

"You should be glad I'm working on it then."

"Never too late, I always say."

Norah forced herself to smile. "So tell me again why you think you don't need help with certain issues. I know you were neglected in your childhood, you feel like you lack self-confidence, you feel insecure about not having gone to college . . . ."

"That's not your business anymore—nothing in my life is your business!"

Norah said softly, "But if you never work it out . . . ."

It wasn't so much that Bet despised the notion of therapy but that she feared it. She always pictured it like a photograph she'd once seen in *Life* magazine of a flood. A little girl sat perched on the roof of a house, holding her doll. All around her was water and more roof tops and chimneys. A helicopter was coming to get her, a tiny helicopter far off on the horizon. But all around her the water was rising; the helicopter would never get there in time. She would have been better off trying to save herself.

"I have my own ways of working things out," Bet said stubbornly. "And besides, I hate that phrase—it reminds me of aerobics and Jane Fonda—which fits, I guess, because it's the same kind of people who do both."

"Well, a mediator isn't the same as a therapist. A mediator would just be for our business stuff. She'd listen to us and help us talk to each other." Norah seemed to be waiting for Bet to make another cynical remark; when Bet didn't she went on, encouraged, "It wouldn't be anyone who knew us and knew our history. It would have to be someone outside our circle, someone who's a trained counselor, a professional . . . ."

"No," said Bet. "Spare me a professional. And why not someone who knows us and cares about us?"

"There's nobody who isn't sick of us and our problems and who doesn't have an opinion about what we've done wrong!"

They stared at each other and had to laugh. "We can't have done everything wrong," said Bet. "Not if we stayed together as long as we did." She meant it as a joke, but tears welled up in Norah's eyes.

"It's just that I can't believe you want to leave the business. We started it together, we did everything together, we made it what it is. It's part of us, and it won't be the same if you go."

"Norah," said Bet exhaustedly. "I can't work with you anymore. Not since we stopped being lovers."

"But," Norah choked, and the tears ran down her face. "You wouldn't want to be lovers anymore anyway. You have someone else, your sex partner you think is so great."

"I don't want to talk about her."

Norah kept crying. "Sometimes I wish we could just go back to how we were. It's so hard with Eleanor sometimes. I feel like she thinks she knows everything, that we're competing. You were never like that, Bet."

Bet sat there feeling nothing, ice down to the bottom. She couldn't allow herself to think about going back to Norah, about even suggesting it. When she did speak, her voice was dry and quiet.

"What about Sylvia as a mediator? She knows us and she cares, but she's never taken a side."

Norah looked up sharply. "Not Sylvia."

"Then I won't do it."

"But Bet, that's like going back to . . . nursery school."

"I don't care."

Norah sat in silence a moment. "I don't know what you see in her. She's just a lonely busybody who wants to be everyone's mother."

"Norah, she *knows* us."

Norah sighed and finished her beer. She put on her beret and looked as if she were going to get up and leave. Then she said, "But you would talk then? If it were Sylvia?"

"Yes," said Bet.

♦ ♦ ♦

The mediation took place on Thursday evening, at Sylvia's house. Norah had called her; Bet didn't know what they said, but it was obvious from the outset that Sylvia was taking it seriously.

She had pushed back the sofa and chairs in the living room and brought in fat velvet pillows for the floor. On a low table she'd placed candles, a pot of tea and a plate of brownies. She was wearing one of her embroidered western shirts and her gray hair had just been cut, a little too short, giving her squarish face a military look. She took off her big watch and placed it on the table in front of them, along with a notebook, the pages of which had been ruled down the middle.

They sat down on the pillows and had some tea and brownies, just as they had so many times in the past. I never really appreciated it then, Bet thought—then she remembered how much she *had* appreciated it, how aware she'd been, so many times, of being safe, loved, protected. She suddenly found it difficult to look at Norah, who was splendidly turned out in a close-fitting brown jacket and pleated men's trousers from the forties. She wore a red scarf around her throat and large round red earrings. Her irrepressible hair formed a bouquet around her narrow oval face.

"Let's get going," Bet said.

Sylvia picked up her pen and waited.

Norah said, at first hesitantly and then with greater firmness, "I thought maybe the way we could do this is that we could each tell how we got into the business, how we feel about it, and how we feel about our lives and how we feel about working with each other . . . and also, how we feel about not working together anymore."

Sylvia raised an eyebrow at her watch and poured herself another cup of tea. "What would you like to talk about, Bet? The same thing, more, less, anything different?"

"I—I'd like to talk about sex."

There was a brief silence and then Norah said, "Oh great. Well, we might as well go right home then."

"Why is business more important than sex?"

"Because we're supposed to have our differences over the business being mediated, so we can work together, that's why!"

Norah glared at Bet. Bet didn't say anything more.

Sylvia had written the words "work" on Norah's side of the page and "sex" on Bet's.

"What exactly did you want to discuss about sex, Bet?" she asked delicately.

"Well . . . I'm interested in how Norah and Eleanor do it."

"Oh my god, I can't believe it." Norah had flushed a dark and angry red.

Sylvia sipped at her tea, doing her best not to look too amused. "What does this have to do with you and Norah, Bet? Isn't it her own business?"

"I've gotten curious, that's all. Not just about Eleanor, as a matter of fact, but about all of them. I mean, in all those years, and with all the talking we did about your lovers, we never talked about what you actually did with them in bed. I tried to imagine it sometimes, but I don't think I was really able to visualize you going down on some other woman. It was always this emotional thing, like I would picture you looking deep into her eyes and kissing her passionately, and I would have this horrible sick feeling of being betrayed. But I never really thought about if you liked them better sexually, or if you did different things, or if you even came with them."

Norah was inflamed with anger. "That's right, throw it in my face all over again. I had affairs, I needed other people, I wasn't just content having sex with you, I got attracted to other women."

"Yes, but what was sex like? That's what I'm asking. I mean, when I first met you you didn't come at all, and then you could only come when you'd had some wine, and then you learned to come with a vibrator, and then you learned to use fantasy . . . but did that work the same way with Joan, for instance? Did you have to go through the whole learning pattern again or did you just come, just like that?"

"You are so fucking condescending, you have always been so fucking condescending about my sexuality. You always acted like you felt sorry for me, you were so concerned I wasn't having your kind of orgasms. Not everybody is like you, you know, so methodical about the whole thing—you'd always be ready and get yourself placed just right, what you thought was the best way, and then you'd just move around a little and come like that. What's so great about that, it's just some animal response—it didn't shake you up at all. Oh, that was nice, you'd always say. And you wanted me to be exactly the same."

"That's not true. I wanted to be with you anyway you wanted."

"But I could never tell you what I wanted, not really. And anyway, I didn't want to tell you what I needed. I wanted to find somebody who knew, who knew what I wanted without me saying anything."

"And did you?"

"Yes!"

"Which one?"

Norah was triumphant now and Bet was furious, sickly green jealousy rushing before her eyes like water drowning her.

Sylvia tapped her tea cup with her spoon. "Girls, girls," she said soothingly. "Let's have some more tea and a minute of silence, then we'll start over."

Neither Norah or Bet looked at each other. If Eleanor is the one who knows without asking, I'll kill her, thought Bet.

"I know feelings are still running strong," said Sylvia. "But it's occurred to me to ask you if this discussion is still relevant. Since you're not lovers any longer and, I assume, have no intention of getting back together. I mean, you both have other interests—presumably you're finding ways to relate to other women sexually . . . ."

"I just resent Norah thinking that you can compare a ten year long sexual relationship, which naturally has its highs and lows, to some brief roll in the hay with someone who's practically a stranger."

Norah glared at her, but said nothing. She was like the good student, who, even though provoked, won't go against the teacher's order to behave.

Sylvia said, "Maybe we could get back to the subject of working together at the store. That's a big issue too, right? And maybe not quite so volatile?"

Norah smoothed down her hair as if she could smooth down her mood. "I feel this . . . session . . . has gotten off to a bad start, but I just want to say—I've been experiencing a lot of grieving about Bet leaving the business. I feel scared about taking it over myself and resentful of Bet for being free of it. This is childish, but I've been reacting against paying her money for her share so she can go off and travel and enjoy herself. And then, I don't know, maybe I'm having some kind of mid-life crisis . . . I feel like, whoa, how did I get into this after all, is this really what I want to do with my life? Do I want to own a futon shop for the next thirty years? It was different when Bet and I started it, you know, we were young, we knew nothing, it was hard to get off the ground. And we were so into it—we slept and ate futons, you remember. Then a couple of years ago it really started to stabilize and I thought, now's the time to try something new, you know, with the imports . . . I've been all excited about it, but now Bet wants to leave, and it just doesn't seem so interesting anymore. I'm afraid somehow . . . ."

And tears filled Norah's eyes.

It incensed Bet that Sylvia looked sympathetic. It was all bullshit, what Norah was saying. "I've been experiencing a lot of grieving"—what kind of English was that? It was therapy talk, that's all. Why not just say you felt bummed out? Not that she really believed Norah anyway. Norah was the one who had made the business what it was and Norah would be the one to continue it. She'd give up the futons in a few years and spend all her time in Japan and China scouting for wonderful new imports. She wouldn't have Bet holding her back any longer; she'd be freer than Bet, making lots of money, traveling all over the world. Bet was the one who should be afraid—she didn't even have a college diploma!

"Do you have a response to that, Bet?" Sylvia asked.

"I guess . . . I'm just wondering whether Norah has ever been interested in an equal relationship, in bed or out, or whether she really prefers to be swept up by some aggressive woman and carried off."

"That sounds more like you and that Kelly person than me and Eleanor. If you want to talk about sex so much, then what's it like with her? Where do you do your fucking—on her motorcycle?"

Sylvia held up two pacific but warning hands. "I did not agree to become a sex counselor for my two good friends, but to help them see if they could work together for a few more weeks and come to an amiable parting of the ways." She looked at them sternly and then laughed. "What about another brownie?"

Both Norah and Bet shook their heads.

"I don't feel up to talking anymore," said Norah. "It just seems impossible to get through to Bet. She hasn't forgiven me for Eleanor and she's going to punish me by leaving the business. It's as simple as that."

"Maybe if you say it often enough it'll become true," said Bet.

"What I don't understand is how you two stayed together for ten years without killing each other."

"Because we loved each other," said Norah, her eyes brimming over with tears. "And it wasn't because of Eleanor I left Bet."

"And it's not because of Eleanor I'm leaving the store," said Bet.

"Well, if it's not because of this Eleanor woman, then why was it and why is it?" demanded Sylvia, a little wearily.

Norah got up, burst into tears, and walked out the door.

Sylvia looked at Bet, who remained sitting, immovable and exhausted. "Well?" she asked.

But Bet just shook her head.

·*13*·

IT WAS CHRISTMAS DAY. THE SNOW HAD ALL MELTED, BUT THE
sun hadn't come out for a week. The sky remained the color of pale granite, with dark purple clouds outlined in
light mauve. Norah was in Portland with Eleanor and her
parents and Bet was at home still reading about the siege
of Leningrad, in the winter of 1940. She was starting to
read some of her books over again, because she couldn't
be bothered to go to the library.

*But gradually the pain faded into quiet despondency,
a gloom that had no ending, a weakness that advanced
with frightening rapidity. What you did yesterday you
could not do today. You found yourself surrounded by
obstacles too difficult to overcome. The steps were too
steep to climb. The wood was too hard to chop, the shelf
too high to reach, the toilet too difficult to clean. Each
day the weakness grew. But awareness did not decline.*

You saw yourself from a distance. You knew what was happening but you could not halt it. You saw your body changing, the legs wasting to toothpicks, the arms vanishing, the breasts turning into empty bags.

The doorbell rang; she knew it was Kelly. Hastily Bet ran to the bathroom and brushed her hair, splashed her face with water. A terrible happiness overcame her.

"Hi!" said Judy Journeywomon nervously. "Mind if I stop in and say hello?" She was wearing a purple and pink knitted cap with short flaps like puppy ears, a thick sweater decorated with bits of twigs and leaves and very worn Birkenstock sandals. She had a canvas backpack with a sleeping bag in her arms.

Silently Bet opened the door wider and let Judy pass inside.

"I thought you might be with your family," Judy said. "I just thought I'd check. I was just passing through Seattle, I just thought I'd drop in and wish you a Merry Christmas, Hannukah, Solstice, whatever. I can go if you want . . . ."

"No . . . I . . . Would you like some tea or coffee?"

"That would be *great.*"

If it had really been Kelly Bet would have been embarrassed by the state of the living room. The books piled everywhere. The unwashed dishes. The half-closed drapes, the stale air, the feeling of carelessness and despondency.

Judy threw herself into the armchair, upsetting the books balanced on the arm.

"I've just worked myself into a corner," she said, picking up Vera Inber and the *900 Days* without paying much attention. "Is Re-Education possible or isn't it? Can you ever unlearn Plastic Passions—or do they just follow you around, wherever you go?"

"It depends," said Bet, rescuing the books from Judy. "What are they?"

"Pseudo-feelings: anxiety, depression, hostility, bitterness, resentment, frustration, things like that, things that just get in the *way*." Judy gave a dry laugh of self-mockery and despair. "But I still can't help having them."

"I thought your book was about tenure or something—in women's studies?" Bet said helplessly.

"One chapter of the book's about that—if I can figure out what I want to say." Judy had taken off her purple and pink cap and her black hair clung tenderly to her head. She looked like a new-born colt, long-limbed and bewildered. "Tenure comes from the Latin, you know. *Tenere*: the act, right, manner or term of holding something. Webster's suggests property or position or an office—I'm maintaining it's the State of Fixocracy, the futile phantom of failed feelings." She suddenly burst out, "It's all Jocelyn's fault. I mean, if she hadn't dumped me I wouldn't have been so vulnerable . . . and now Mary Anne . . . I don't have anybody . . . I have to work at that stupid deli and I'm stuck on an island in the middle of nowhere. I just *had* to get out this morning. I woke up and *had* to leave and—"

"Judy," Bet interrupted her. "Where are you passing through *to*?"

Judy fumbled with her cap as if she were afraid of being thrown out. She looked mournfully at Bet. "I'd been planning to visit this friend of mine in Eugene for weeks. Then, this morning, I decided I would . . . but I've sort of lost momentum. It seemed like an adventure but I got scared when I got to Seattle. It's so quiet out there on the streets . . . and then I remembered that you lived here. I even remembered your last name, Gallagher, so I looked in the phone book and got your address. I hope you don't mind."

Bet looked at the books in her hands and suddenly couldn't understand why she was reading them on Christmas. "No," she said finally. "I guess I don't mind."

She took Judy over to Sylvia's; she couldn't think what else to do with her. She had no knack for helping other people through their troubles—she couldn't even help herself. She was a whole rubbish heap of nonbiodegradable Plastic Passions.

"We'll just drop by and see what she's up to, whether she's got other company or what."

But it appeared that Sylvia wasn't celebrating the holiday at all. She came to the door with a small tacking hammer in one hand and a width of brocade in the other. The house radiated the sound of country western. She didn't look especially pleased to see them.

"Where's your son? The grandchildren and all that?" Bet asked in surprise. "I thought the house would be swarming."

"They all took off for Hawaii this year. Since they saw me for Thanksgiving I guess they figured that was enough." Sylvia shrugged. Her short gray hair was slightly ruffled; her mouth pursed as if she were holding small upholstery nails. She didn't look like the good-natured former landlady Bet had described to Judy, but now Bet, embarrassed, couldn't give up.

"What about Lou and Janine? Your other friends?"

"You want a run-down? Lou and Janine are in Philadelphia with Lou's parents. Nancy and Kathleen are in Northern California at a Buddhist retreat; Paula and Deb are up in the mountains skiing. Various other people are visiting various other families around the country, or having various winter holidays with their loved ones."

"Oh."

"Don't look so sad. This is the first Christmas *you've* ever stayed in Seattle."

There was something at once sour and resigned about Sylvia's expression. The voice of Waylon Jennings twanged out around them and Sylvia didn't invite them in. Clearly she was wishing they would go away and leave her in peace.

But Bet couldn't leave now. "I hope you don't mind, that Judy—this is Judy Journeywomon—and I stopped by. Maybe I could—take us all out to dinner or something."

"Eat out on Christmas Day, Bet?" Sylvia shook her head. "No thanks."

"Well, okay, maybe not," said Bet, backing away, suddenly close to tears. What a bad friend she had been to Sylvia, never bothering to ask her what she was doing for the holidays, if she needed any company. And here she was again, coming empty-handed to her door, needy and importunate.

"It's easy enough to make something here, Bet," Sylvia said in a gentler voice, placing a hand on Bet's shoulder, making her turn and face her. "But you'll have to help."

"I know," said Bet. "I want to."

"I'll help too," Judy piped up, with an admiring look at Sylvia.

They were playing Monopoly very companionably after dinner when the phone rang.

"It's for you, Bet," said Sylvia.

She still thought it could be Kelly.

"Hi," said Norah. "I wondered if you might be there."

"Oh. Yeah . . . where else? We're just playing Monopoly."

"You and Sylvia and . . . "

"And Judy, one of the women from the island. I've mentioned her once or twice."

"The feminist scholar."

They laughed, but Bet heard Norah's anxiety. "I think she has a crush on Sylvia," Bet said.

"Oh, everybody does," said Norah crisply, but she was relieved. She hesitated. "I'm still here in Portland."

"I guessed. Having a good time?"

"Oh . . . well . . . " Norah paused. It was unclear whether she'd called to say this or whether it just came out. "Eleanor and I aren't really getting along. I mean, it's impossible just to hang out. I feel like I always have to be saying something interesting or provocative, or we have to be running around looking at things all the time. I mean, there aren't that many things in Portland to look at!" Norah gave a forced laugh. "I shouldn't really be telling you all this, I guess."

"I don't mind. What are friends for?" But then Bet couldn't help herself. "If Eleanor doesn't work out—"

"Oh, that's okay, Bet," Norah said hastily.

"I just meant—there are a lot of other fish in the sea."

"I'm complaining—not fishing," said Norah, and tried to laugh. "Sorry, it's so boring. What about you and Kelly?"

"Oh, that was no big thing, I mean, it was fun sexually . . . ."

There was a long pause, one that couldn't really be filled.

"I guess I'd better go," said Bet at length. "They're waiting for me to land on their hotels."

"You're playing Monopoly, huh?" Norah tried for a lighter tone; she didn't seem to want to say good-bye. "I remember all those games we used to play with Sylvia—Monopoly, Parcheesi, Clue—god, I remember we even had pillow fights . . . and remember that time, once, we'd eaten dinner in the backyard and after we finished, we threw all the plates and bowls and salt and pepper shakers and glasses off the table, into the bushes, we were being so silly, we were laughing so hard and we didn't even know why."

They laughed again now, but Norah laughed harder. Bet's heart had crumpled up like a kite that has been flying through empty space and has just landed in some trees.

"Norah," she said. "I really have to go. But listen, I'm glad you called. I want to stay in touch. I do."

"This isn't the *end*." Norah turned all panicky. "I mean, we've still got another week of work together."

"I haven't forgotten," said Bet.

"Well, just checking."

Bet didn't want to play Monopoly anymore.

"You mind if I go out to the cottage for a few minutes?" she asked Sylvia.

"Extra key's on the ledge as usual."

It was twilight, blue cold twilight, outside Sylvia's back door. The cold snap had broken; familiar wintry dankness had moved in again. Clouds massed overhead, dull violet sponges soaking and squeezing. The earth was soft again after the snow, chill and moist, like something left in the refrigerator too long.

In the garden everything colorful was gone; only green and gray and brown plants kept watch through the winter months. The climbing roses around the cottage were thornily protective of the walls.

Bet felt immensely old. It must be longer than five years since she'd left the cottage. It felt like centuries, another life. The door creaked as she went in. It never used to creak.

The walls had been blue; they'd had radical posters and women's posters and Japanese design posters; they'd even had a small reproduction of Vermeer's *Girl with a Pearl Earring* because Norah thought it looked like Bet.

That had been in the early days.

No, it wasn't as nice now as when she and Norah had lived here, even though Lou and Janine were clearly better off. They had a big color TV and a VCR, a Macintosh, a Cuisinart. Their furniture was modular, upholstered in bright ticking. Everything else was plastic in designer shades of rose and aqua.

Before she'd moved in with Norah she'd never felt she had a home, it was that simple. She wasn't supposed to put things on the wall in her bedroom when she was growing up; it made holes in the wallpaper. She wasn't supposed to sit on her bed: "Beds are for sleeping, Betty!" She wasn't supposed to leave things lying around. She didn't have many things to leave around.

After high school she'd defiantly lived in squalor for a while, loving it. She never made her bed, picked up her clothes or washed a dish if she could help it. She'd been asked to leave a group house once, for ignoring the chore list.

Norah used to lecture her, "I'm not naturally a neat person either, but if we're going to live together there has to be *some* order. Maybe you'll feel differently when we have our own place."

Bet *had* felt differently. They had scavenged furniture at garage sales and Goodwill, varnished it, painted it. They had sewed and swept and dusted and endlessly arranged their little nest like model homemakers.

And the whole time Bet had been under the impression that Norah was making a home for her. Not that they were both doing it for each other.

"Aren't you going to turn the lights on, Bet?" Sylvia's voice was soft behind her. She had a Coleman lantern in her hand; she set it down on the coffee table.

"I was just thinking . . . ."

Sylvia sat down across from her, more tentative than usual. It came to Bet that they didn't know their roles with each other anymore. Always before when Sylvia had come out to the cottage it had been to hear how Bet and Norah were doing, if they needed anything at the store, or did they have anything white to add to her laundry load.

"Thinking . . . about Norah?"

"Did I ever tell you how we met?

"Probably. Tell me again though."

"We were in a cooking class together. Through the Experimental College."

"That's right," said Sylvia. "Wasn't it bread or something?"

"Croissants," said Bet. "It was an all day workshop."

"I knew it was something yeasty."

"I thought she was such a knockout," said Bet. "I couldn't understand why everyone in the room wasn't staring at her. She had her hair really long then, and with that olive skin and those gold hoop earrings—she looked like a gypsy—she was wearing a smock, white with blue embroidery, and she never spilled a thing on it . . . . I couldn't figure her out, why she kept looking at me. After a while I couldn't concentrate. I didn't know what the hell I was doing there anyway. I'd wanted to take an all day auto mechanics class, but I'd put the number down wrong. Then I thought croissants might come in useful sometime . . . . I wanted to say something to Norah, wanted to ask her out for coffee afterwards . . . . But this guy came to pick her up who looked just like her. 'Is that your brother?' I asked her . . . . And can you believe it, she said yes. She thought I was a separatist because I was wearing overalls and she didn't want me to think she was straight. That was what she said later anyway. She said she was attracted to me because I followed the teacher's instructions so methodically. She said that proved I was a sensible person, and she wanted someone sensible after Daniel. She liked it that I was quiet, and that I had a sense of humor."

"Nancy liked my laugh," said Sylvia.

The light in the room softened Sylvia's angular face and flickered on the surface of her glasses. Had she even been listening to Bet? She said, "It's kept coming back to me today that it's seventeen years since I left her."

When Sylvia was feeling good she called her Nancy the Nurse and told Bet stories of Nancy's missionary zeal to reform her. She'd gotten Sylvia out of the bars, made her stop smoking, urged her to take up a hobby, any hobby—like upholstery. But when Sylvia was feeling glum, Nancy became a symbol of a happier time.

"I was only thirty-two, for christssakes," Sylvia said now. "I thought I had great new opportunities for relationships in front of me. I did—it's just that they only lasted about seven and half weeks average . . . well, except for Deana, that dragged on for a year or so. At first it was exciting, now I can't take it, can't take that little gleam in Judy's eyes, for instance. I sometimes think, even if the relationship with Nancy seemed boring, at least we really loved each other."

"Well, you're still friends," Bet offered. She didn't like to hear Sylvia talking this way.

"Yeah, she and Kathleen have been my friends for fifteen years. They used to refer to me as the gay bachelor. Now they just feel sorry for me."

"You really think that you and Nancy could have made it, could still be happy after all these years? Wouldn't you have missed finding out all you did find out? I mean, whether the affairs lasted or not?"

"Once I would have said yes, breaking up was worth it, because of what I did learn. But when I think of the next twenty or thirty years alone . . . ."

Bet couldn't bear to think of it; she took Sylvia's neat strong hands in her own. "You're not *alone*."

Sylvia squeezed her hands and suddenly a wild idea popped into Bet's mind: she and Sylvia, peacefully and contentedly living with each other into the future, Sylvia doing her upholstery, Bet doing—something—neither of them having affairs, devoted and committed . . . .

"Forget it, Bet," said Sylvia. "I want you as a friend, so don't get that look on your face. Do your experimenting elsewhere. What happened to Kelly anyway?"

"She chose the orange that wasn't as thick-skinned."

"It would never have worked. Just from the way you described it."

"Sylvia—did you ever think of me and Norah as butch and femme?"

"I don't know," said Sylvia. "Maybe."

"Which were we?"

"You were you. And Norah was Norah."

"I guess that was the trouble, wasn't it?"

There was a pause, then Sylvia asked, "Are you sorry about Kelly?"

"I don't know . . . it's like it took over my life, like I wanted it to. Nothing would have happened if she hadn't pursued me. It made me feel wanted again." Bet stopped and involuntarily her hands clenched over Sylvia's, as if she were falling. "I guess it felt like it was filling up the empty space that Norah left, but what happened was, it just made the space more empty. Do you know what I mean?"

"Yes."

They sat holding hands for a while. It was very cold.

"What's Judy doing anyway?" Bet asked.

"Calling her mother. I told her to."

"Good old Sylvia—why can't you tell me what to do?"

"I have told you, Bet. The same thing I tell myself: Forget and move on. Forget and move on."

"And does it work?"

"The moving on part does. You can't help it."

"But the forgetting . . . ?"

Sylvia stood up and pulled Bet to her feet. For a moment they remained there silently, hands clasped, in the middle of the cottage. The light from the Coleman lantern played on the unfamiliar objects, but when Bet closed her eyes she smelled the cottage as it had been, a long time ago, when she and Norah lived here.

Then they heard Judy calling from the back porch, "Sylvia? Bet?" and they broke away from each other and started to the door.

When she heard the hinges creak behind her, Bet knew she would never go back inside again.

·14·

SHE DREAMED SHE WAS IN A EUROPEAN CITY, A CITY THAT WAS like a mouthful of broken teeth. Building after building bombed, windows in shards in the street with pathetic bits of ordinary life—shreds of flowered curtain and smashed pieces of pottery —all mixed up with twisted metal and burning wood. She was standing on the sidewalk in front of the place she'd been living, looking through piles and piles of rubble. She tore at it, threw it behind her, she was looking for something familiar, something that would remind her of Norah. Up and down the block there were other people doing the same thing: she saw Kelly and Sylvia, she saw her own mother. They were all looking for someone or something underneath the wreckage.

Finally, at the bottom of a pile of smoking debris she found a little Japanese lacquered box, one that had belonged to Norah. Inside it was a note that said "I love you."

At first Bet was touched and tremendously relieved: here was proof that Norah loved her and only her, proof that she was alive. Then suddenly she realized it was no proof at all, it could have been written to anyone. She knelt there for what seemed a long while, looking at the note, and every moment she became more and more convinced that Norah was dead, that Norah had died in the bombing.

She decided that she had to tell her parents what had happened. With the beautiful lacquered box holding Norah's message in her hand and with snow falling all around her she began walking. The snow fell faster and faster, and the cold grew inside her like a cancer. Her fingers grew so numb they could hardly grip the box; finally it fell from her hand and was immediately buried by the snow.

Bet kept walking; she was in a long line of people, all wearing shawls and torn jackets, all with their heads bent, marching like a black line of ants through the snow; they were starving and they had all lost somebody, and as they walked they keened. Louder and louder until their voices filled the sky with loss and mourning.

After a while the snow stopped and Bet found herself standing in front of the house where she'd grown up. There was the scraggly hedge, the picture window in the front with the faded drapes, the once bright, now tarnished brass mailbox that said "Letters for the Gallaghers."

Sylvia was in the living room, feet up on the coffee table, reading the paper. "Why, Bet, how nice to see you, good day at school? Norah's not here, but she'll be home soon. Come in and sit down."

But Bet couldn't move from the doorway. There was something wrong about this, she knew it even in the dream. She wasn't really in high school any more and Sylvia wasn't her mother. She had come to tell her mother about Norah, but she realized her mother didn't even know about Norah and her, didn't know that Bet and Norah had been lovers for ten years.

It was as if she had gone back in time, and she knew the future but Sylvia didn't, and didn't have any idea either what was going to happen. She didn't know there was going to be a war, and that Norah would die and that everything familiar was going to be bombed into tiny little pieces that could never be put together again.

And for a long time, in the dream, Bet stood in the doorway of the house where she'd grown up, looking at Sylvia with her feet up on the coffee table, with a feeling of sadness and loss that was as immense as anything she'd ever felt, and Sylvia kept looking at her and saying the same thing over and over, "Why Bet, how nice to see you. Why don't you come in and sit down?"

Judy slept late on the sofa in the living room. Over a cup of tea she told Bet reluctantly, wistfully, "I don't think I'm going to make it to Eugene. I guess I'll head back home . . . "

But Bet couldn't bear to be alone. "I'll drive you," she offered.

There was no real sun by the time they started, after lunch. The sky was a tattered laundry basket of gray and faded dishtowels and gauze curtains. For miles the black-green firs crept close to the highway, as if lonely for company, even when they reached the Skagit Valley and the horizon opened up, the color of the day didn't change. The land and trees and farmhouses kept absorbing light, stuffing themselves with light, giving nothing off.

Bet had thought she'd never drive this way again. This highway was as familiar to her as the contours of a body. The landscape spoke of expectations never realized, anger never expressed, grief never named.

They talked at length about Judy. Judy's family. Judy's first lovers in high school—her English teacher and then her English teacher's roommate. Jocelyn. Mary Anne. Agonizing analyses that went on for ten and fifteen minutes at a time. And then, "What do you think I should have done, what should I do?"

No one had ever asked Bet for her advice except Norah, who usually ignored it. She tried, "Maybe you should live by yourself in the city for a while. Maybe you should go back to school, do graduate work. Or you could travel somewhere, live in another country . . . ."

Rotely she suggested alternatives, but while Judy was talking, her mind kept stumbling over memories, like a long rocky road she had traveled in bare feet. She saw herself at eight, the silent child who played by herself and obeyed her parents unquestioningly; at fourteen the sulky adolescent who had one or two friends at school, who sat dreamily through her classes and did badly on tests; at eighteen the stubborn graduate who moved away from home and never looked back. She saw herself before she met Norah, a quiet, cautious woman who worked for other people, who spent evenings alone reading or taking walks, a woman so out of touch with herself that she didn't even know she was unhappy.

"But I can't decide whether to keep going in women's studies—because I'd keep running into Jocelyn and her girlfriend—or just do something completely different. I don't know—like forestry . . . ."

"You should probably stick with something that feeds you intellectually," Bet said, watching the road.

Judy gave her a grateful look. "It just helps so much to be affirmed in my commitment, to know that somebody believes I have an important contribution to make. The thing I like about you, you're a supportive person. You give me a peaceful sense, like you're self-contained and can take care of yourself. You—and Sylvia's like that too."

"Well, thank you," said Bet, taken aback.

"You underestimate yourself," said Norah once. "You don't understand why I love you at all."

And it was true, Bet never really had understood why Norah stayed with her, year after year. Norah could have had anyone; she chose Bet. At least sometimes.

She remembered Norah shouting at her during their first fight, a year or so after they met, "Don't you have any ambition? Do you want to work for some jerk all your life?"

Put like that, of course not. But before Norah challenged her, Bet had been perfectly content. It was Norah who always wanted more: more money, more action, more women, more life. She was never satisfied, she was always afraid of failure. Once she said, joking, to Sylvia, "I don't understand it, *I'm* the one with the big mouth, all the ideas, the chuzpah, but if it weren't for Bet, we wouldn't really have gotten anywhere with this business."

And Sylvia had laughed her booming laugh, that made Norah wince, and said, "I'm glad you see that, Norah. I hope you always do."

♦ ♦ ♦

"I thought when I moved to the island," said Judy as they turned off I-5 for Anacortes, "that I was moving to a kind of Gynutopia. A woman I met at NWSA told me there were lots of lesbians there into spirituality, rituals, remembering. I don't know what I expected. I really think I must have been imagining some kind of Greek city-state, white columns, reflecting pools, women in togas lounging around discussing philosophy . . . ."

"What, here in the Northwest?" Bet was jolted out of her thoughts.

"Not *literally*," Judy said, with her dry little laugh. "You know what I mean though. And why not? You have to have a vision that keeps you going . . . my vision has always been of women together making something of their lives, I can't be more definite than that at the moment. I believe it has something to do with education, reeducation, teaching each other and ourselves . . . but I was disappointed."

"By the lack of reflecting pools?"

"By the level of discourse."

Bet agreed. "It's fairly low in this part of the universe."

"I'm too romantic, that's the trouble," Judy said meditatively. "I get involved with women who are completely wrong for me. When I think about Jocelyn and Mary Anne they seem so different, but in lots of ways they were the same. They pretended to think I was wonderful, then they dropped me for someone else."

"Maybe you should try a lover closer to your age," suggested Bet.

"But that's the trouble," said Judy. "They don't attract me. I want someone who's *lived*." She paused. "Someone like Sylvia."

"I wouldn't get your hopes up," said Bet.

They stood on the deck as the ferry crossed to the island. The world was a monochromatic study in gray: wave, forest, cloud.

Judy had her cap back on and was breathing deeply, leaning against the railing, looking out. Her cheeks reddened in the wind, her lovely mouth was set in thought. In spite of her introspective mood she seemed exuberantly healthy. "There's a kind of shallowness in women's relationships, don't you think?" she asked after a while. "We get so easily attached—there's this merging, where you don't know who you are—but our reasons for falling in love are so arbitrary, they're not based on intellect, on the passionate exchange of ideas."

"Sometimes," said Bet. "Sometimes they're shallow, yes."

"Take me," said Judy. "I fell in love with Jocelyn who seemed so brilliant, so wise. But what did we really have in common? She was ambitious in an ordinary way—she didn't really want anything more than equality with men. And then there's Mary Anne." Judy sighed. "She thought I wanted mothering. But all I wanted was an older lover." She broke off. "I really miss her."

Bet said nothing, she looked at the island which was steadily getting larger, like a great gray-green beast getting up on its knees, shaking off the mist around its shoulders.

Judy stared at it too. "I wonder how many lovers I'll end up having in my life. Once I thought Jocelyn and I would live together forever. I had it all pictured. A house in the country, a huge library, both of us publishing books on important feminist issues . . . I didn't think that way about Mary Anne, but I still loved her. Now I wonder . . . I wonder what I'm supposed to be learning."

"What you need to, I suppose."

Judy looked at her as if she'd said something profound. Bet had to laugh. "Now don't ask me any more questions. I don't understand love or desire any better than you do. Until a few months ago I thought . . . Now I'm completely starting over. I'm just like you."

Judy took her hand. "You say you don't understand," she said. "But I know you do."

They arrived on the island about four-thirty. The road to Judy's wound through stands of second-growth alder and hemlock, delicate and gray as cobwebs. The road was gravel and not well kept up. Within the woods, in a clearing, were a large house and three smaller ones. Judy's cabin was a little farther off. Judy began to forge a path through the underbrush. It was raining now and the wet leaves and branches caught at Bet's clothes and slapped her face. Darkness was beginning to fall. She couldn't help thinking about how close Kelly was.

"There's the outhouse. And a treehouse for the summer. The tipi is meant for ceremonies, but we don't seem to have them. And here's mine."

It was a square shack made of wood, with one small-paned window. A claustrophobic feeling came over Bet as they squeezed inside, but she felt too tired to make excuses and leave again. It seemed darker in the woods than it really was; it was as if she had become enmeshed in a fairytale.

Judy was eager and pleased. "You're my first real visitor." She lit two or three candles around the room and plumped up the bed. "Get under the covers," she urged. "You'll be warmer."

The room, illuminated by candlelight, was not as small as it looked from the outside. There was a walnut table and some pine shelves filled with books and papers. Around the bed ran a single shelf covered with shells and crystals and smooth flat stones. The silence was stupefying.

"I can't stay long," Bet said, sitting down on the bed. "I'll take the next ferry."

Judy's face fell, but she moved quickly around, lighting a small oil stove and putting water on. "Get inside and get warm," she urged again, and pulled the covers back. The bed was heaped with quilts and comforters and stale old pillows smelling of massage oil.

Bet sighed and got under the covers. It *was* freezing, and she was so tired, so unbearably tired all of a sudden.

"Isn't that nice and warm?" Bet couldn't keep her eyes open. All around her mists of patchouli incense began to rise, while the pillow was deeply impregnated with clove. It was greasy, strange and irresistible.

"I'm going to give you a massage," Judy announced. "That's something I'm really good at."

"I've got to go soon, I mean it," murmured Bet, and then drifted off again.

The water boiled and Judy removed the kettle, then threw tea leaves into a pot. She grabbed a bottle of clove scented massage oil and crawled in bed on top of Bet, straddling her back. It was all very quick, though Bet protested. Judy pulled off Bet's sweater and tee-shirt and squirted oil on her shoulders.

With forceful strokes she pressed down along the spine.

"Ow!" said Bet. "I mean, that feels good."

"I didn't mean to sound so discouraged on the ferry," Judy said. "I'm *not* discouraged. I believe in women creating the future. We *have* to—before men destroy everything."

She pounded on Bet's back.

"How?" gasped Bet. "I mean, what kind of future?"

"That's what we have to discover," said Judy. "We have to be Bold Voyagers. We can't give up just because some woman dumps us." She cracked Bet's spine. "We can't let our vision of an Amazon reality be overthrown just because some women are petty and shallow and cruel."

Bet's teeth rattled as Judy lifted her head and then pushed it forcefully into the greasy clove pillow. "Hey, let up," she managed. "I'm with you. Against cruelty."

Judy subsided into a more rhythmic pummeling. "When my book comes out, then she'll be sorry," she said almost cheerfully. "I mean, then she'll *see*. How my private loss was transmuted into a quest for higher truths . . . of course I'm not totally ruling out graduate school . . . ."

Norah had last massaged her at the Japanese inn. Her small neat hands were good at it; she wasn't as rough as

Judy. She massaged like a lover, her fingers becoming part of Bet's back.

"When we get home," she had said. "Let's start over. I mean it. Buy a house, start a garden, we've never really had a garden. I'd like to do something, I don't know—big—with you."

"Isn't the business big enough?"

"You know what I mean, Bet." And Norah had leaned her face down to where she was massaging the shoulder blades, so it was as if she were speaking directly to Bet's heart. "I'd like to, you know, put some of the past away, do things differently."

Did she mean she wouldn't have any more lovers? Bet was afraid to ask, for fear that Norah would get defensive and that the mood would be broken.

She said cautiously, "Things are pretty good the way they are . . . maybe we don't need a house just yet."

Norah's touch faltered imperceptibly, then she continued her massage. "I wish," she said finally, almost to herself.

"What?"

"I wish we had some more tea, don't you? Shall I call the waitress?"

"Are you wishing I wanted a house with you? I do wish that—someday. There are other things I wish now . . . ." She didn't finish and Norah didn't ask. Instead she said,

"No. You're right about the house. It's too soon. We don't have the money, you're right." Norah stroked the skin of her back softly. "You're always the sensible one, my Bet."

♦ ♦ ♦

Bet woke up in pitch blackness, needing to pee. Judy lay naked next to her in the oily clove sheets. Her body felt young and resilient; Bet pushed it gently away and stood up.

It was cold and she stumbled, trying to find her sweater, but Judy didn't stir. Bet creaked open the door and squeezed outside. In the moonlight her watch said it was just after nine.

And suddenly, anguish seized her. Grief for everything and everyone she'd ever lost. It came at her like a grizzly out of the forest, knocked her down, ripped her flesh, tore out her heart triumphantly and ate it.

Bet ran to get away from her panic. For a few minutes she charged blindly through the sopping wet underbrush, breathing hard, weeping.

Then, just as suddenly, the feeling passed. She was standing in a small wet clearing ringed by lacy trees. Above her the sky moved like a river cloudy with froth, breaking on stars. The moon was a floating white candle stub, bobbing and shining.

She had to see Kelly. Hear her explanations, find out what it had all meant to her. They couldn't just end it so abruptly.

Bet found the gravel road and started walking down it. Behind her, from the main house, she heard the fire sputtering in the chimney, the drowsy sound of women's voices.

Mary Anne's farm was on a slight rise. The lighted windows of the house looked like different sized jars of clover honey and pear preserves arranged on two unseen shelves. As she approached the house there came the sound of a voice, piercing and bewildered with love and sorrow. Leontyne Price again. "Addio, mio dolce amor." From inside the barn came contrapuntal sounds of clanking and soft lowing. Bet imagined the six ungainly cows in their stalls, chewing and mulling it over. They were so patient and steady they didn't have, couldn't have human counterparts.

Bet crept closer to the buildings. None of the curtains were drawn against the night, the house seemed so full of light and radiance that it had to pour out into the world, make its luminous stand against all the forces of the dark. Bet hung on the fence, unable to think what to do next. She felt so shut out; it was as if she were paralyzed, watching.

She saw Mary Anne sail across the kitchen window and Kelly follow her. Mary Anne's hair was coppery under the light; her teeth were white against her freckles. Kelly looked like she'd just come out of the shower; her hair was flattened and her ears stuck out. She came just to the top of Mary Anne's shoulder. They laughed and then Kelly caught at Mary Anne's arm and pulled her close. There was such tenderness in Kelly's gesture that Bet almost cried out.

Why had it never occured to her that Mary Anne and Kelly could really love each other?

There was a voice in the barn. A steady murmur that underlay the ringing soprano from the house. Bet climbed over the fence and crossed to stand by the barn window.

" . . . So then I'm going to have real boots, those kind with inlays, colored leather. And a leather saddle, probably with turquoise and silver I think. So then we'll sign up for the race and nobody will know who we are. We'll be mysterious, coming out of nowhere, and boy will they be surprised when they see us . . . .They'll all say they haven't heard of such a thing—a twelve year old girl riding a big race and winning . . . maybe I'll be thirteen by then . . . ."

There was a sound of hooves shifting on straw, the quiet listening breath of the horse. The voice went on rhythmically and lovingly. "All I want sometimes is to get on your back and ride far far away, away from Mom and her girlfriends and even Kelly and home and everything I know. Ride really fast and fly over the fences and the bushes, faster than anyone has ever gone before. We would be like a brush fire, or the north wind—we'd go so fast no one would ever see us—they'd feel a little breeze and say, 'Was that Tam and Nutmeg?' "

She paused and laughed a delighted and confidential laugh. "Was that Tam and Nutmeg? But only we would know."

Bet didn't go to the door of the house and bang on it, didn't stand outside shouting Kelly's name, demanding explanations, apologies or remorse. She didn't offer apologies or explanations of her own. Instead she turned away, thinking of Sylvia, and she thought, I will take my share of the money from the business and buy a house.

I will buy a house of my own and never again stand outside looking in.

♦ ♦ ♦

The moon was brightening overhead, tossing off its wraps of navy and gray chiffon. The air was wet but fresh, and smelled of the earth, of the old fall leaves underfoot. There was no one else about. Only Bet, walking on gravel, surrounded by pastures and trees.

For now, only Bet.

When she and Norah were in Japan Norah had insisted they climb Mount Fuji. Bet hadn't wanted to.

"I hate to climb uphill, you know that. I always hate it."

"But you always like it when you get to the top."

"No I don't. *You* do."

"Oh Bet, come on. Mount Fuji!"

They had started at Kawaguchiko Fifth Stage, amidst the souvenir shops and restaurants. It was early September but still sticky and humid. The trail was steep and rocky and packed with other hikers, even though the season was over.

After about two hours Bet announced she couldn't go on; she was turning back.

"I'll pull you," said Norah, holding out a hand. Her face was rosy and her hair was sticking in tendrils to her damp forehead.

She pulled Bet up over a hard bit, and then they climbed on. After another hour or so, Bet said, "Norah, I can't. Really. I'm dying. I don't want to, it's not worth it."

"Don't give up, we're two-thirds there," said Norah. "I'll push you."

She ran behind Bet and pushed with her hands, then turned her back, and back on back, pushed Bet up up, over another especially steep part.

An hour from the top, Bet said, "This is it. I can't. I really can't," and Norah said, "All right. But I'm going up." And she ran past Bet on her way to the summit.

Freed of Norah's presence, her pushing and her cajoling, her example and her will, Bet immediately sat down on a rock and looked out. There was no landscape, no vista, only roiling white clouds as far as she could see. It was cooler here, a faint breeze ruffled her hair. For a long time she continued to feel Norah's back on hers. She knew that she would never have gotten even this far if Norah hadn't pulled and pushed her.

And all the same, this was as far as she'd wanted to go.

Bet reached the turn off to Judy's commune, and then the driveway. She'd say good-bye—and thank you—or perhaps she'd just leave a note. If she hurried she could catch the eleven o'clock ferry and be home by two.

"Oh Norah," she couldn't help saying aloud.

And that was when Bet began, knowingly, to grieve.

About the type:
The text of this book was set in ITC Garamond, 11 point on 14. It was composed by Alef Type and Design, Los Angeles, California, and Irish Setter, Portland, Oregon. The book was printed by McNaughton & Gunn, Saline, Michigan, on acid-free paper.

Also by Alexander McCall Smith

No. 1 Ladies' Detective Agency Series

...ssor Dr Moritz-Maria von Igelfeld Series

Sunday Philosophy Club Series

DRE

Prof

44 Scotland Street Series

44 Scotland Street
Espresso Tales
Love Over Scotland

Short Stories

Heavenly Date: And Other Flirtations
The Girl Who Married a Lion
The Baboons Who Went This Way and That

Myths are universal and timeless stories that reflect and shape our lives — they explore our desires, our fears, our longings, and provide narratives that remind us what it means to be human. *The Myths* series brings together some of the world's finest writers, each of whom has retold a myth in a contemporary and memorable way. Authors in the series also include: Chinua Achebe, Margaret Atwood, Karen Armstrong, AS Byatt, David Grossman, Milton Hatoum, Natsuo Kirino, Victor Pelevin, Ali Smith, Donna Tartt, Su Tong and Jeanette Winterson.

DREAM ANGUS

The Celtic God of Dreams

Alexander McCall Smith

Alfred A. Knopf Canada

PUBLISHED BY ALFRED A. KNOPF CANADA

Copyright © 2006 Alexander McCall Smith
Published by agreement with Canongate Books Ltd., Edinburgh, Scotland

Library and Archives Canada Cataloguing in Publication
McCall Smith, Alexander, 1948–
        Dream Angus / Alexander McCall Smith.
(The myths series)

ISBN-13: 978-0-676-97873-5
ISBN-10: 0-676-97873-8

I. Title. II. Series: McCall Smith, Alexander, 1948– . Myths series.

PR6063.C326D74 2006   823'.914   C2006-902596-7

First Edition

Designed by Pentagram
Typeset in Van Dijck by Palimpsest Book Production Ltd., Grangemouth,
Stirlingshire

Printed and bound in the United States of America

10 9 8 7 6 5 4 3 2 1

For Malcolm and Nicola Wood

CONTENTS

Introduction

This story is a retelling of the myth of Angus, a popular and attractive figure of the Celtic mythology of Ireland and Scotland. Angus is a giver of dreams, an Eros, a figure of youth. He comes down to us from Irish mythology, but he is encountered, too, in Celtic Scotland. He is a benign figure – handsome and playful – who in modern times has inspired not only the poem of W.B. Yeats, 'The Song of Wandering Aengus', but also the lilting Scottish lullaby, 'Dream Angus'.

In this version of the story of Angus, although I have taken some liberties with the original, I have tried to maintain the central features of Angus's life as these are revealed to us in the Irish mythological sources. These sources, though, do not provide much detail, and so I have imagined what his mother, Boann, might be like; I have interpreted the character of his father, the Dagda, in a particular way and have deprived him of the definite article that precedes his name; I have assumed that

Bodb was rather overbearing. Purists may object to this, but myths live, and are there to be played with. At the same time, it is important to remind readers of the fact that if they want the medieval versions, unsullied by twenty-first-century inter-polation, they still exist, and are accessible. We must bear in mind, however, that those earlier texts are themselves reworked versions of things passed from mouth to mouth, embroidered and mixed up in the process. Myth is a cloud based upon a shadow based upon the movement of the breeze.

Celtic mythology is a rich and entrancing world, peopled by both mortals and gods. It embraces the notion of parallel universes, the real world and the otherworld. There are signs of the otherworld in the real world – mounds, hills and loughs – and the location of mythical places is frequently tied to real geographical features. It is no respecter of chronology, though, even if the later Irish heroic tales claim to have happened at a particular time in history. Angus belongs to the early body of stories – stories of a time beyond concrete memory.

★   ★   ★

In retelling the story of Angus, I have brought him into the modern world in a series of connected stories which for the most part take place in modern Scotland. The part played by Angus, or the Angus figure, in each of these, may be elusive, but such a figure is present in each of them. Unlike some mythical figures, Angus does no particular moral or didactic work: he is really about dreams and about love – two things that have always had their mysteries for people. Angus puts us in touch with our dreams – those entities which Auden described so beautifully in his Freud poem as the creatures of the night that are waiting for us, that need our recognition. But Angus does more than that: he represents youth and the intense, passionate love that we might experience when we are young but which we might still try to remember as age creeps up. Age and experience might make us sombre and cautious, but there is always an Angus within us – Angus the dreamer.

Alexander McCall Smith, 2006